BLOOD AT DUSK

DARK INK TATTOO
BOOK TWO

CASSIE ALEXANDER

Copyright © 2021 by Cassie Alexander
All rights reserved.

No part of this publication may be reproduced, distributed, or transmitted in any form
or by any means, including photocopying, recording, or other electronic or mechanical
methods, without the prior written permission of the publisher, except in the case of
brief quotations embodied in critical reviews and certain other noncommercial uses
permitted by copyright law.

This is a work of fiction. Names, characters, places, and incidents are a product of the
author's imagination. Locales and public names are sometimes used for atmospheric
purposes. Any resemblance to actual people, living or dead, or to businesses, companies,
events, institutions, or locales is completely coincidental.

WWW.CASSIEALEXANDER.COM

COVER BY THE BOOKBRANDER.
INTERIOR ART BY FRANKIE.
USED WITH PERMISSION.

INTRODUCTION & CHARACTER ART

Angela: I thought my best friend Willa was crazy when she wanted us to flirt with the leader of a motorcycle gang but somehow, the three of us fell in love...at least that's what I thought. Then I realized the horrific truth about Gray's gang—everyone in it was a werewolf. Monsters were real. And suddenly, Willa and I were expendable, unless we became monsters, too.

Jack: I wasn't expecting to see my high school crush at a strip club— but once I saw Thea spinning around a pole, I knew I'd gamble everything I owned for a night with her. Too bad in order to save her, I would have to make a deal with a vampire: become a monster, or watch Thea die.

She was a woman forced to sacrifice her humanity.
He was a man risking everything for first love.

Welcome to Dark Ink Tattoo, where needles aren't the only things that bite....

Dark Ink Tattoo is a scorching paranormal in the vein of Sons of Anarchy, with strong sexual situations and bisexual MCs.

Content warnings can be found on cassiealexander.com.

CHAPTER ONE
JACK

W hile your teenaged fantasies oftentimes involve bumping into teachers, former babysitters, and/or high-school head cheerleaders at the strip club, none of them—no matter how detailed—can prepare you for when it happens in real life. Which is why I was staring slack-jawed at Dorothy—*Thea*—as Bruce punched me in the arm.

"Jesus, when's the last time you saw a naked girl, Jack?"

I waved him away and kept staring. The runway was a long thing, phallically shaped, and we were at the tip of it while she was stage center near the pole, far enough away that it both could-and-couldn't be her simultaneously, like some Schrodingerian dream.

Bruce grabbed my head and yanked it near so he wouldn't have to shout over the music the club pumped in. "You're embarrassing yourself—and me."

She walked around the pole, looking out into likely darkness since all the lights were aimed at her, making all the sequins on her white bikini glint—it was like she was blindingly beautiful, too pretty to even see properly. Then she lunged forward and in, lifting herself up, long legs pointed in a dramatically suggestive V, ending in two glittering red platform heels, all the better to walk down a pornographic yellow brick road.

I turned toward him without taking my eyes off her. "I know her."

"The fuck you do."

But I did. I had a sudden flash of smoke and damage, a crinkle of red metal peeled up like wrapping paper on both sides of a tree and me running down to rescue her from the passenger side of a BMW, as quarterback Duncan Beamm staggered out on the driver side to puke, from a likely BAL of 0.3 and a head contusion.

Everything afterward...

"We're in Vegas. Bet me," I told Bruce, as she began a slow turn.

"A hundred."

"Done," I said. "Go hit the ATM."

He snorted and didn't move. Thea spun, the muscles of her arms, her stomach, the swing of her legs, making her swirl like a slow carousel. What was it like being up there with everyone watching? Rowdier groups of men waved fistfuls of cash, shouting lewd suggestions, and she ignored them, intent on her own internal metronome, letting the music move her. When it came time for her to take off her top it seemed natural and she swung down dramatically, one leg curving up to brace against the pole, the pink perfection of her nipples on display, swaying with the music like twin poppies.

How many times in high school had I desperately wanted to see those breasts—to touch them? The closest I'd ever come was that day in the rain, holding her to my chest, blood streaming out of a small cut on her cheek.

"Thea? Thea? Are you okay?"

I was the first on the scene—they'd slalomed past me in the rain for no reason, and fishtailed over the edge of the road. I'd called it in on my way down the hill, leaving my truck parked on the shoulder up above for the ambulance to see.

I heard the sound of another puke on Duncan's side as Thea's eyelids fluttered. She sat up and took everything in then looked up at me.

"He has scholarships," she said, having done a mental calculation at the speed of light, far faster than I would've been able to.

"So?"

"Say I was driving."

"You weren't. He was, and he's an asshole." There were beer cans on the floor of her car, I could see them through the open door, beneath the fluttering tatters of airbags.

"Babe!" Duncan bellowed on the far side. "Babe, where'd you go?"

Thea wriggled free and stood with me close behind. "I'm here, baby, hang on—" she shouted, then turned to me. "Please, Jack."

We'd been in a few classes together, on and off, a group project here or there, but we both knew where we belonged. I was with the kids the other kids hated, the ones that listened to the wrong music and couldn't afford nice clothes, whereas Thea was some sort of angel, so light the rest of the cheerleading team picked her up to make her fly.

"Fuck his scholarships, Thea—he almost killed you."

She put her hands on my chest. "I know, okay? But it was an accident—and my dad's gonna kill me over this already—there's no reason to ruin his life too."

I had no love for Duncan or anyone else on the football team. But for Thea? I'd spent four years watching her in the halls, loving the way her skirts grazed the edges of the dress code, the way the Texas sun brought out tank tops that sometimes slipped to reveal brightly colored bras. I knew all of her classes after lunch and could identify her laugh at a hundred paces. And while I knew I could never be with her—I knew how high school worked, and those of us on the outside of it had a very clear view of the inside—there was no way I could deny her now.

"Babe!" Duncan shouted, finally standing higher than the hood, holding one hand to his head, reaching out to her with the other. "Come here, get away from that loser—"

"Shut up Duncan!" she shouted back, looking at me with tears welling in her eyes. We heard a siren in the distance and I stepped away from her.

"Only because you're asking." I jerked my chin at Duncan. "Fuck him."

"Fuck you," Duncan bellowed, charging two steps forward before toppling over.

She ran to his side, kneeling down, and then looked up at me. "Thank you," she whispered. I shrugged my shoulder like it didn't matter. The second the cops got there, I told them my story and drove off.

The next two weeks of school held a strange kind of magic for me. I'd see her in the halls, and she wouldn't look away. She gave me shy smiles, finally, at long last, noticing me—and making me feel that it was okay for me to notice her. She even came over and spoke to me at my locker, asking how I was doing, and we talked for long enough that one of my fellow 'losers' noticed and interrogated me afterwards.

But the week after that, a mere month before graduation, Duncan started a rumor that I'd driven them off the road—all the better excuse for half the football team to viciously beat me. I didn't dare go back to school, much less graduate—I left high school and that fucking small town and I never looked back.

THE TEMPO of the music changed as Thea took another turn. I didn't know how to feel, watching her. My blood was rushing south but my mind was confused. We'd never talked again after I'd quit school—I heard she'd left town to go try to make it in LA. I never really knew if she'd egged Duncan on or if she'd told him the truth.

When the song was finished she let herself down gracefully, one long leg after the next and stalked the perimeter of the stage, still topless. Unlike the girls who crawled up and down it, flapping their asses for cash, she didn't seem to care if you paid her—she stared down shadowed men, daring them to have watched her without offering up money, like a goddess expecting tribute.

And when she reached the end of the stage and us—I leaned forward into the light, holding a twenty. Seeing me, she jerked back in surprise as her face lit up with recognition. "Jack?"

"Hey—" I began, wanting to call her by her real name, but I stopped myself in time because I didn't know if that was cool.

She shook her head at my twenty, refusing it, then kept walking down the line, slightly faster.

"That was Ruby! Let's give Ruby a round of applause!"

Applause smattered and then the cranking rhythm of the next dancer's song overwhelmed it.

"SEE?" I told Bruce, watching her walk away.

"Yeah, yeah," he said, grunting as he pushed himself away from his spot to get my hundred. He'd give me shit for it later but he was a man of his word. That's why I worked for him, back in Dallas, in a small tattoo shop near Deep Ellum. We were in Las Vegas this week to mostly be in Vegas, vaguely attending a tattoo convention as an excuse to write off our vacation.

This was our third night in town. We only had two left and I hadn't really wanted to come here but Bruce had and now—*Thea*. I watched the place she'd walked off stage like a cat watched a mouse hole, willing her to return. If she did though, what would I say? *Hey, remember that time I lied for you and then got three broken ribs for it?* Did her parents know she was here? What about the rest of our classmates? We were only five years out of high school, but as big as Texas was, gossip still travelled fast.

I was still staring at the stage door when a shy hand tapped my shoulder. "Jack?"

I turned and there she was. Her blonde hair cascaded in waves past her shoulders and black eye-liner winged out over each of her blue eyes. She was wearing a shiny white coat that matched the bikini underneath, and her lips looked like she'd kissed red glitter. "Thea—wow. I would've never guessed I'd run into you here."

She laughed coyly, ducking her hair down to twirl a lock of it. "I know, right? Small world."

"Definitely."

She looked me up and down from underneath impossibly long eyelashes. "You've filled out."

I'd been a scrawny punk in high school—but time at the gym and a late hit from puberty had fixed that. "Yeah, and you got taller," I teased, since her shoes added six inches to her, easy. She laughed—and I couldn't stop looking at her. So much of her was on display, and the memory of her half-naked spinning, merging into all my other high school fantasies.... "You're just as gorgeous as I remembered."

Under the fake red light above I thought I saw a deeper flush. "Aw, thanks Jack."

"How did you get here? Last I heard you were moving to LA—can I get you a drink?" I knew strippers worked on some sort of drink system—I didn't want my curiosity to cost her.

"You're not...mad at me?"

She looked so fragile in that moment and whether it was for real or for show, I answered honestly. "No. Not anymore."

Thea gave me a relieved smile, red lips stretched wide. "Then a Jack and Coke, please."

"Sure thing."

I left and returned with her drink, likely all Diet Coke since the bartenders were on the girls' side, and my drink, definitely straight Coke—I'd already had enough to drink tonight. She was mirage-like enough, I didn't want alcohol to make the memories fade. She was still standing, although there were a few empty tables, then I realized the problem. Strippers weren't allowed to actually sit with customers—only sit on them. As I tried to figure out how to navigate that, Bruce returned with my hundred and gave us both a once-over.

"Do I give this to you or do I give it to her?" he asked with a sly grin.

Thea answered before I could. "Him. I might want the chance to earn it out of him later."

"So be it," he said, sliding the bill in-between my fingers and the sweating glass. "I'm old and poor and going to bed—unless you've got a sister?"

"Fresh out, I'm afraid," Thea said with her slight Texan drawl.

"Damn," Bruce cursed, and then gave me a 'Don't screw this up' clap on the shoulder before walking toward the door, leaving me alone with her.

"Is there somewhere...real we can go?" I asked.

Her red lips twisted, acknowledging how hard it was to get to reality from here. "Yeah. But I'm afraid I'm gonna need that hundred."

I gave it to her without thinking and let her lead me into the back.

THEA PULLED ME IN, sauntering—I wondered if it was possible not to saunter in those heels—until we walked past a very large Samoan man and into a private room. It held a smaller central stage, but you could tuck into any of ten different booths along the walls here for private shows, each separated from the rest by glittering curtains providing the illusion of privacy. She drew me into one of these and ran back out, leaving me looking at an empty brass pole before darting back in.

"Sorry—the cash—it was to bribe him not to bust us," she said with a head tilt toward the muscle and then she sat beside me.

"Then it was well spent." I offered her her drink and she took it. "Soooo…" I began, drawing the word out.

"Soooo…" she said, mimicking me. "Are you okay? I—I always wanted to ask, but the longer I waited the harder it was and so I guess I just gave up." Her shoulders slumped.

"You knew what happened?" I'd always wondered if she had—and if she was somehow on Duncan's side.

She caught one of my hands with both her own. "I told him not to. I even broke up with him. But that just made him angrier and I didn't know what to do."

I looked down at the hand she held, the oddity of her unmarked flesh so close to mine. "I don't think you could've changed anything, Thea. Besides, by then I was pretty used to getting beat up."

She winced. "I'm so sorry, Jack. If I'd known—"

"It's fine." I lifted my hand, breaking the contact between us. True, I'd been angry for a long time afterwards—but in the scope of things, it was just one more thing to add to my list. I'd been an angry kid. "How was LA?"

Thea brought her hands demurely back to one knee. "Hard. Harder than this, if you can believe that." She recrossed her legs and I tried to ignore the way her coat rode up. "High school was such a breeze, I just thought I'd be able to go out there and conquer the world, you know? Waitress some, audition some, and then eventually someone would pick me."

"How could they not?"

"Jack," she said. "Shush."

I inhaled to remind her of how locally famous she'd been, back in the day—and then realized it wasn't likely to help anything, and actually might hurt her feelings. My defense mechanism had always been not to have dreams, all the better to never have them crushed—but she had, and they had been.

She took a sip of her drink. "The only guys who wanted to take me seriously were the ones who wanted to sleep with me. At least out here I get paid if they think like that."

"Yeah," I said softly, agreeing, because I didn't know what else to do.

"What about you? What brings you here?" Her voice was perky again. I could feel her putting her sexy armor back on and would do just about anything for her not to.

"The usual. After high school my folks kicked me out and I made some bad decisions, until I wound up in Dallas and started working at Bruce's shop."

"Doing?"

"Tattoos." I was wearing a long sleeved button down shirt and went for my throat, undoing the first few buttons quickly, revealing the head of the dragon that curled up from my chest and over my shoulder.

Thea looked amused. "That's a change."

"What is?"

"A guy taking off his clothes for me."

I laughed. "What should I charge you?" I asked, flipping my collar back and forth dramatically. She giggled as I buttoned my shirt back up. "This is Bruce's—kind of an initiation. He won't let you tattoo anywhere on someone else that you don't have one first. But I've done tons of them now—I've got pictures on my phone if you want to see." Anything to keep talking to her.

"Sure," she said, leaning in.

I pulled my phone out and thumbed through them, telling her each one's story—why the person had gotten it, what'd made it memorable or hard—tattoos I hadn't quite talked people out of, the ones I actually had.

"So you didn't just take their money?"

"I did a few times. But if I'm not good at something—or if their urge to have all of their children's faces inside a kaleidoscope on their navel is incurable—I send them elsewhere."

"That's good," she said. "You're a gentleman."

"Heh." With the thoughts I was having about her now, I wasn't sure that I qualified. But I smiled down at her—now that we were seated, she was the height that I remembered—and she smiled back until she saw something that I didn't see and leapt into my lap, startling me.

The golden curtain parted and a beautiful dark-skinned woman leaned in. "Ruby?"

"Yes, Miss Rosalie?" Thea asked, twisting back toward her, while grinding against me. Her arms were in a tangle around my neck, and I could smell her so clearly, soap and a floral shampoo mixed with healthy sweat from dancing.

The dark woman gave me a piercing look and spoke with a French accent. "Are you a satisfied customer?" she asked. Her words practically compelled an answer.

"Yes. Of course," I answered honestly, then glanced at Thea. All her wriggling was making me hard—I hoped to hell she didn't notice. An uncontrollable dick in high school was one thing, but now I was a grown man. "With her, who wouldn't be?"

Her lips pursed and she gave Thea a *look*. "Don't take your job here for granted, just because of your connections."

"I wouldn't dare," Thea said.

"You'd best not," she said and pulled back, leaving the shimmering curtain shaking behind. I exhaled a breath I hadn't realized I was holding.

"How can someone so pretty be so frightening?" Thea wondered aloud.

I had so many answers for that right now, but she turned towards me before I could say anything. "Sorry, that was my boss," she said, bouncing off of me to stand.

As for me, it was too late. Despite all my best intentions and thinking of anything but her butt, she'd given me a raging hard on—

and she knew it. She probably had a telepathic sense for them, a kind of professional ESP.

"Sorry. Not always such a gentleman," I apologized.

The corners of her sparkling lips pulled up into a conquering smile. "A gentleman doesn't have to be a saint."

Before I could ask her what that meant—if anything—she took a step away. "Rosalie's right—I've got to get back out there, you know how it is."

"Yeah, totally." I stood and nodded eagerly, taking my out. "It was good seeing you, Thea."

"You too, Jack." Her accent had been crawling back all evening, as if brought out by my own. "I miss Texas out here."

"Hell, I've only been here for three days, and I miss it."

"You won't say, uh..." she said with a shrug, to indicate the rest of everything.

"Not a word." The few friends I'd stayed in touch with after high school, either they wouldn't believe me or they didn't deserve to know. I reached out and pulled the curtain aside, and she seemed surprised.

"Ladies first," I explained.

"Thanks," she said, giving me a genuine smile, then walked out back into the bar.

I INHALED DEEPLY and followed her at a respectful distance. Who would've thought I'd have a more meaningful conversation with the object of my teenaged lust at a strip club than I'd managed through-out all of high school? And gotten a kind of closure for one of the worst periods in my life? That'd been a hundred dollars well spent. With the money I hadn't given other strippers while talking to Thea, I had plenty left for a ride. As I neared the door I cast back one last look, hoping to see Thea there somewhere, even if it was with another guy—when a different girl teetered up.

"I'm sorry, I'm leaving." I held up my hands like she was a mugger.

"I know—take this," she said, handing me a slip of paper. I took it from her and walked out into the night, unfolding it under a sign with the club's name: *Vermillion*. And just when I thought the night couldn't get any more unbelievable, it did.

3346 Brandlin Way, Apt D, 5 AM—T

CHAPTER TWO
JACK

I went to a diner, my mind reeling. Why would Thea want to see me? I knew what I hoped—and I knew what I shouldn't be hoping, at the same time. Still though, God, at the thought of those legs that'd wrapped around that pole, wrapping around me instead? An urgent, almost electric, need flowed through my body from stem to stern.

I texted Bruce to let him know that I might not see him until late tomorrow. He was still awake, probably in the bowels of a casino, and he texted me back a high-five. At about four thirty I caught another ride and wound up standing outside of what I could only assume was Thea's apartment building by 4:45. To pace or not to pace, that was the question. I didn't want anyone to call me in as a possible burglar but I also didn't want to be waiting right outside her door.

The arrival of a small four-door made everything moot as Thea got out of it and grinned at me. "Eager much?"

"Politely punctual," I said, smiling back. She was wearing slip-ons, a tank top, and yoga pants now, hauling all of her stripper gear in a huge duffle bag at her side. "Can I take that?"

"Please," she said, handing it over to me. "God, how I have missed southern men."

"Is it all that different out here? Or just an occupational hazard?"

"Bit of both, I suppose," she said, as I followed her up a flight of stairs outdoors. She unlocked her door and let me in.

Her apartment was cozy, full of warm-colored overstuffed furniture and a nice entertainment system. "Make yourself at home," she said, before taking her bag from me and disappearing into the back, where I assumed her bedroom was. I heard water running and sat down on her couch. I currently had a strange definition of home, sleeping in a closet-like studio over the tattoo shop—I preferred this one much more to that.

"There," she announced, returning without make-up and her hair back in a tousled bun. "Sorry if the magic's gone."

"Hardly," I said. If anything, her willingness to be casual amplified it.

She walked past me and into her kitchen, opening the fridge up. "It's not too late, is it?" she asked, leaning over the door to offer me a beer.

"Haven't you already had forty of those tonight?"

"Ha. Only if apple juice counts as whiskey."

"Then I'll take one." She brought it back to me and sat on the end of the couch, close enough to touch, but still far away enough to make it hard.

"Thanks," I said. I popped my beer open and looked around again at the room and then her, trying to hide my frank disbelief that I was here and that this was happening. "How'd the rest of your night go?"

Thea looked surprised. "You really want to know?"

"Yeah. What's it like? I mean I knew you always loved to dance—"

"Yeah." She gave her beer a shy look. "It's—it's different then what you see on TV. No one shows the back stage stuff. My boss—well, you saw her. She's her own kind of scary. But I guess you have to be when half the girls are high—there's so much bullshit back stage." She took a long swig of her beer, definitely her first of the evening. "Girls arguing about which guys are their marks—which songs belong to them—figuring out which girls are desperate enough to work a group before Rosalie assigns you anyhow—it's a lot of drama. But where else can you make a couple hundred bucks a night with no degree?"

"Tattooing? But only if you're very, very good, and lucky, and willing to work every Friday and Saturday and your clients are smart enough to leave tips."

"Oh my God. Clients," she said, making air-quotes around the word. "This guy tonight tried to show me photos of his wife and kids."

I sputtered the sip of beer I'd been taking. "What the *fuck*?"

"I know, right? Sometimes they just want to pay you to listen about their day. If you're topless, all the better."

"You'd think therapy would be cheaper and smell less like cherry lotion."

She laughed. "Also, like come on. We're covered in glitter! If you're going home and your wife still does your laundry, she either knows and doesn't care, or she's got her own thing on the side."

"Maybe they just 'lose' their luggage at the airport before they go home."

"Maybe," she said with a grin, then shook her head. "I can't believe that you're not mad at me, Jack."

"I'm not exactly a zen monk—but all that was in the past. I like who I am now. I wouldn't change a thing."

I didn't know it was true until I'd spoken the words, but it was. Ever since Bruce'd taken me under his wing, I had cash on hand and a way to get more. Even better, I had respect, from others and from myself, something high school had been far better at taking away from me than creating.

Thea sank back into her couch. "Man, if I could go back—there's so much I would change."

"Like what?" I asked.

She looked over at me. "You really want to know?"

"Of course," I answered, then added, "I want to know everything you're thinking." I felt foolish for saying it the second the words left my mouth, but it was too late at night for me to be on my guard, and I'd meant it besides. I'd wanted to know what was going on inside Thea's head since seventh grade at least.

Instead of laughing as I instantly feared, she seemed taken aback, and I watched her set her drink down in a deliberate fashion, before reaching up to undo her bun, like the 'librarian' in so many music videos. "I would change this," she said, crawling over the distance between us on her couch.

I stayed still as the answer to a thousand teenaged prayers unspooled like a film reel in my mind. She was on all fours, and came close enough I could feel her breath. "I never should've," she started to apologize—the apology that I'd waited years for, only now I didn't want to hear it. I leaned forward and kissed her instead.

Her lips were as soft as I'd always dreamed they'd be. My head tilted and she leaned in. It was natural for our lips to part, for our tongues to taste, and I reached a tentative hand up to touch her cheek as she crawled forward, moving to sit in my lap.

There was no way not to be hard. Years of watching her, and all the events of tonight—no amount of thinking about baseball or horror films could cure me. I wound my hands around her waist, finding where her shirt ended to touch silky skin—but I needed to ask where this was going before we went on. I pulled my head back, taking her lower-lip with me in between my teeth, tugging her closer to me as her hands ran up my chest and neck and into my hair to keep me close.

"Do you fuck as good as you kiss?" she whispered.

"Absolutely. But," I said, and she leaned back, her beautiful lips pulling into a pout. "I don't want apology sex, Thea. So if that's what this is, it's late—let me go home and jerk off in peace."

She gave me a thoughtful look and then moved in a very conscious way, grinding slowly against me, relishing taking the power I pretended to have over myself back. "Is 'friend I haven't seen in a few years' sex okay? Or what about 'sex with hot guy who turns me on?'"

"Either of those will do," I said, and caught her hair with one hand, while I sent the other underneath her shirt. I wound her hair into my fist and pulled her mouth to mine again. Her hands fluttered for a second—then started undoing the buttons at my neck, as my other hand sank under the elastic of her bra and reached beneath, bunching up her shirt, so my thumb could graze her nipple. "Too much clothing," I complained, releasing her hair and pulling up her shirt as she twisted to let me, and then she was sitting half-naked on my lap. I was awestruck by her, for a second—and then I brought my hands up to maul her, firmly grasping every piece of her lovely smooth skin I could touch—then I bowed her forward so that I could kiss her, from her collar bone down—I had to taste her breasts, it was an animalistic urge.

She moaned as my mouth reached her nipple and she played one hand in my hair—the other she tried to shove between us, to get further down my chest, at what was hidden in my jeans. I sucked on her and nuzzled her with my now 5-am-o-clock shadow, trying to eat her, smell her, feel her all at once. Her nipples went hard and I gently bit one while pulling at the other.

"Oh, yeah," she breathed, and I felt her hips rise as her ass clenched against my thighs, as though she were fucking an imaginary cock.

I was dying to give her the real thing—but I wanted to give her so much more, first. "Stand up."

"What?" She lolled forward, eyes a little cloudy.

"Stand up and take those pants off."

She made a disappointed groan but then got up and stood a few feet away. "These pants?" she said, hitching her thumbs into the waistband.

"You heard me," I said.

She turned so her ass was facing me and looked over her shoulder. "Are you sure?" she asked, pressing them slowly down, revealing an inch of creamy skin and the beginnings of a pink thong.

"Very," I said, in a tone that broached no teasing.

She swung her hips from side to side, slippery-slipping them off as slowly as she could.

"All the way?" she asked, bending forward, so that I could see the satin veiled promise between her thighs.

"Everything," I commanded.

She took her time with the thong, making the moment last—then turned around more slowly, shyly, to show her body off. She was small and tight and only the thinnest line of fur ran down toward her clit like a suggestive arrow—like her body already knew exactly what I meant to do to her.

"C'mere," I said, gesturing her closer. She came nearer—and it took a moment and some manhandling for me to make myself clear, as I made her stand on her couch over me, a foot on either side of my hips, so that the space between her thighs was directly in front of my face.

"Jack—" she breathed.

"Shh—" I said, and anything else I was going to say was buried against her pussy.

Between the softness of the couch and how short she was, she was the perfect height for this—so I leaned in, and felt her brace herself with her hands against the wall above me. Her folds opened for me, already dripping with wetness, it was easy for me to play my tongue in and up, to taste her more. She made a soft noise as I lapped forward and a louder moan as my lips found her clit to suck, rolling my tongue against it.

She thrust then, her dancer's hips giving way, and I followed her with my head. One of her hands came down to grab into my hair as both of mine reached up to cup her perfect ass, all the better to follow it.

I pushed my tongue up, in, out, sucked, again and again, tasting every part of her that I could reach, and then she sped up so fast I couldn't follow and I didn't want to slow her down—I just left my tongue out and let her ride on it, feeling her ass clench and release above me in endless waves.

If she was going to come this way, so be it, but I needed to come too—I let go of her to pull out my cock and started stroking it below her, looking up at her fabulous body, the bottom curve of her breasts, as her head rolled back and—she pushed herself off the wall with obvious effort, to stare down the flat plain of her stomach at me.

"Put a condom on."

"Yes, Ma'am," I said, reaching into the back pocket of my jeans. I'd never pulled one on so fast before, but I was ready as her hips came down.

It was like she was sliding down an imaginary pole. She put both her hands on my shoulders and lowered herself, letting me manage any issues with aiming, while she watched—because she wanted to see the look on my face at the moment when—

"God," I whispered, as my cock dipped inside her.

With a dancer's strength, Thea hovered there, atop me, pulsing up and down, tormenting me with only an inch of her heat, leaving me powerless, willing her to give me more.

Slowly, so slowly, she did, making me appreciate each and every moment of her slide. She was tight around me, I could feel myself filling her, and from the sounds she made I knew she could feel it too. She changed from feet to knees and then we were sealed at the hips, her pussy tight against me, my hard cock buried inside.

"This feels so good," I murmured, cupping her ass to me as I went to kiss her breast.

"I know," she said, "I know." She made a soft sound then and caught her breath, beginning to rock on me.

I tried to thrust—I really did—but the way her eyes closed as her head rolled back and her hips began to pulse—I'd been with enough women to know that sometimes the moment belonged to them, and as she started bouncing I realized there was nothing I should do, could do, except let her use me. I put my hands at her waist and leaned back into her couch to arch up for her pleasure, and as I did that, she opened her eyes.

"Oh—Jack," she whispered, grinding herself against me.

"Fuck yes," I growled, moving my hands to hold her ass tightly.

Her hands clasped my shoulders tight as she started rocking harder, whipping my cock in and out of her with tiny thrusts, making it fill her and then leave her empty. I watched in amazement, but didn't interrupt—it wasn't every day a woman used you this fiercely, and I wanted to let her ride. I could see her winding up to come, in the way her mouth opened, hear it in the roughness of her breath, feel it as her pussy grasped around me.

"Oh, fuck, yes," I breathed, encouraging her, her perfect breasts bobbing. Her stomach curled against mine, grinding her clit into me with each push. I could feel the glory of her ass tightening and pulling—and above all else I could feel her pussy—the pussy that I'd longed to be in, ever since high school, the one I must've stroked myself to a hundred times, imagining being inside at night—it fit my cock like a glove. Every time she squirmed and pulled and pushed and rocked it made me harder and more ready—

"Oh—oh—oh!" she warned, impossibly fast now, squirming atop me, pinned by my cock. I grabbed her hips hard and pulled her toward me, shoving myself deep inside her. "Oh! Yes! Jack!" she said and started shaking, spasming, from her head down to her toes and every part in between—

"God, yes," I growled, as her pussy's waves of orgasm grabbed hold of me. "*Yes.*" I used my hands to make her hips fuck me for another crucial moment and then shot my cum deep with a guttural sound, my own hips rising and falling, making hers ride along, until both our bodies sank.

Thea rocked back, making long sighs of pleasure, still swirling her hips over me, one lazy hand stroking her own breast, until she sat back, moving incrementally until my spent cock slid out. Then she fell over on the couch beside me, seemingly exhausted. "Oh, Jack, if you were that good in high school, I missed out."

"You and a lot of other girls," I said, pulling off the condom as I pushed myself back inside my jeans. I hadn't even gotten to take any of my clothing off—all the better to go stumble out and catch an Uber.

As if reading my mind she rose up on her elbows. "If you think you're going home tonight, tomorrow, whatever the fuck day this is now—you're sadly mistaken."

I stared at her. I'd already lived the dream and made peace with the fact that despite what she'd said it could still be apology sex. But round two wouldn't be, for sure. "Yeah?" I asked her, all of my high school hopes and insecurities rushing up.

She nodded eagerly with a soft smile. "Oh yeah."

CHAPTER THREE
JACK

"Is he going to think you died?" Thea asked from beside me on her bed.

"And gone to heaven." I'd woken up before her and she'd caught me looking at an inquiring text from Bruce on my phone. It was nearly 3 PM, I was starving, and the things we'd done until the mid-morning—it'd take days to air out the scent of sex in the air.

"Don't go," Thea said, rocking up onto her arms beside me with a slight pout.

I shrugged, mystified. "All right." I saw enough of Bruce at work and he was a man, he'd understand. I still had another day off here—did she? "What were your plans?"

"I don't have any. Other than you." She gave me a mischievous grin.

"You don't have to work?"

"Not until midnight. I might need a nap between now and then, but...." One of her hands crept under the sheets to encircle my cock.

I chuckled darkly and lay back. "Has anyone ever told you you're insatiable?"

"You say that like it's a bad thing."

I grinned, even as she was making me hard—teenaged Jack would be so proud. "I'm out of condoms. So unless you've got some, we'll have to face daylight."

She laughed. "I'm a stripper. Strippers burn in the sun, it's why we use tanning beds." She crawled over me suggestively to open up a nightstand drawer full of...things. Things with tassels, things with straps, things that looked like rubber swords, and nubbly things—I leaned over to gawk.

"What are all of those?"

"Gifts from admirers. You would be surprised at all the gifts I get. And also sex toys." Thea gave me a devilish look. "You've never played with anything before?"

"I mean I know what a vibrator is and I've seen raunchy porn, but—"

"You've never seen so many in one space before," she said, gesturing grandly at the drawer, before digging around in it again, pulling one Trojan up in its shining package and moving to all fours. "I think this is our last condom, so we'd better make it count." She batted her eyelashes, the very picture of innocence as she offered the condom over. "What do you want to do with it, Jack?"

It occurred to me then that there was no way I could've possibly explained this exquisite moment to younger-me, to give him hope and something to look forward to. No time capsule, no letter from the future, not even a personal visit would've made him—*me*—believe.

And yet here I was.

"I don't know." I said—because I didn't care. Anything, any way I could get inside her, and make her feel good, make me feel good, was golden.

"Oh, come on Jack—you know."

"Dealer's choice," I said, pushing the condom back. She thoughtfully tapped it against her lips.

"Hmm. It's been awhile, but...." She darted back down and pulled up a toy, a small buzzy thing, then knelt nearby. "When we were younger...you had to have thought about me, right?"

"Uh huh." There was no point in lying.

"Did you ever jerk off while thinking about me?"

"Of course." I snorted. "Just like every other red blooded male in our graduating class."

She leaned forward and pulled the sheet back. "Did you ever think that someday I'd be jerking you off?" she said, leaning over to stroke my cock.

"No," I said, with absolute honesty. The second her hand touched my flesh—I wanted to shudder with excitement. She kept stroking as she lowered herself down bodily, crouching beside me.

"Did you ever think that someday I'd be sucking your cock?" she asked, staring up, as her lips parted to take me in.

My cock had to have been bathed in my cum, we'd fucked four times last night and hadn't showered off—but she didn't seem concerned, and the thought of her lapping up my cum made me even harder.

"Definitely not."

"Hmm," she agreed, swirling her tongue around my head before licking down my shaft to nuzzle at my balls.

"Goddamn," I whispered, and she made another amused sound.

"Last question then—did you ever jerk off imagining yourself fucking me in the ass?"

I startled from the reverie I was falling into. "Uh—no. Not really." And that? Was a lie. But admitting that I had seemed uncouth.

"Why not?" She faked being offended.

"It's, uh, not in my repertoire."

At that, her face lit up. "You've never?"

I hadn't. Imagined it? Yes. Done it? "No. It just...hasn't come up."

"And you've never asked?"

"It seemed better not to know what I was missing."

"Well, you're wrong—and soon you won't be missing it anymore." She dove back into the drawer and pulled out a glove and lube, handing them over to me. "You can't just jump on in there— not with me at least."

"Oh—okay?" I said, pulling a glove on my right hand. I was used to that at least, I wore gloves every day at work.

"Get your fingers all warm and lube-y," she said, and then lay down beside me. I heard her toy turn on, and saw one of her hands dart down beneath her, presumably landing between her thighs.

"And then?" I asked, doing what I was told, rubbing lube between my thumb and two forefingers.

"Go slow," she said, and angled her pert bottom up.

I reached for her with my ungloved hand first, stroking down her back and up her thighs. This...was a change for me. And yet how could I not? Not when she was willing? I trailed my hand back up her leg and then grabbed hold of her left ass cheek, pulling it wide enough for me to see where she wanted me. I stroked a lubed and gloved finger down her crack carefully, then gently pushed in.

She made a happy moan as I felt her ass take me. It felt just like fingers in a pussy, only the walls were tighter. I pushed deeper, and then started playing my finger in and out, back and forth.

"Oh, that's good," she whispered, rocking her ass up to take me, and then back down into her toy, I could hear the intermittent way its buzzing muffled on her skin. "More?" she asked, as I pulled my first finger almost out—and pushed a second one in to join it.

"Ohhhhhhhh," she moaned.

She was so, so tight. But I not only pulled in and out, I spun wider, testing the boundaries of this new place, feeling her asshole soften for me.

"Yeah, Jack," she said, with another appreciative moan. And when she felt wide enough, when I thought I could fit inside—I pulled my hand out, snapped the glove off, and pulled the last condom on.

I was surprised when she rose up to all fours in front of me. "I want you to see it," she said, twisting back as I slicked the condom with lube. "I want you to watch yourself go into me."

What I wanted to tell her was that I'd been going into her ever since I'd first seen her last night—in less than a day, I'd gone into her so hard I might've lost track of myself and fallen in.

"I don't want to watch *me*, Thea" I said, lining myself up behind her. "I want to watch *you*," I said, and pushed forward.

She groaned at the same time I did—the sensation of her ass was unlike any I'd experienced before. I could feel the tight band of muscle there pressing against me, and waited for it to relax so I could push further. As it did, I did, my hands spreading her cheeks wide, feeling myself sliding into her, falling anew.

"Oh Jack—just like that," she whispered softly. I moved forward bodily until I was right behind her, my cock settled deep.

She made a whining sound and started to move, catching herself between her and her toy again, me watching her ride on and off of my cock, feeling how my cock spread her wide. Then I started to thrust, slowly at first, and she stopped for me to find my own rhythm, pulling myself almost out, then watching-feeling myself slide back in.

"That's so good," she purred, darting her hand back to buzz her clit again.

"Give me that," I said, reaching under her to follow her hand, pinning her with my body. She gave it over and I touched it to her, still buzzing. "Here?" I asked, missing on purpose.

She shook her head. "Nuh-uh."

"Here?"

She laughed and shook her head again.

"Here?" I said, winding it up through her folds against her clit.

She whined instead of answering me.

I caught my other arm around her chest and leaned into her, forcing us to fall forward together, me still fucking her, my chest pressed against her back, covering her bodily against her bed.

"I like you here, trapped," I said, kissing her neck as her hips kept pulsing between my cock and where I held her toy. It was like I was taking her from the front and behind both at once. She reached a hand back to run through my hair and started to writhe beneath me, to give me more of her ass, and then grind against the vibrator, back and forth, back and forth.

"I want to feel your ass come around me, Thea," I said, catching her earlobe to suck. "I want you to fuck yourself with my cock until you can't help but come," I whispered. I wanted to do anything, everything, to feel her lose herself again around me.

"I want that too," she whispered—and underneath her my hand found a breast and pinched its nipple and she gasped, as my lips found her neck again. "Jack." Her free hand wound in the sheet beside me, as her other hand reached back to clench in my hair. "This is so good," she moaned.

I utterly agreed with her, and hoped to hell she realized how amazing we were together. I knew I'd be dreaming about the past twenty-four hours for the rest of my life—I wanted to make sure she would, too.

I pulled the toy away from her clit and she made a petulant sound.

"If this is our last condom—I don't want you to come yet—I don't want to stop fucking you," I whispered as I stroked inside her, because it was true.

Her hand in my hair pulled and she twisted to look back at me. "Then don't," she whispered back.

I held her tighter, my arms wrapped around her, one hand against the softness of her breast, the other holding the toy as my thrusts ground her against my knuckles. And I closed my eyes, feeling my cock sink into her, again and again, savoring the delicious tension as it pulled out, the perfect sensation as it pressed back in. How was some other man not here instead of me? How was I the man taking this beautiful woman in her glorious ass? I opened my eyes again and saw her still watching me, knowing that I was only barely still in control, and it was time.

I opened my palm with the toy and planted it against her clit again.

"I'm never going to stop fucking you," I whispered in her ear, and realized it was true—even without her there, from here on out, I'd always be reliving the last night in my mind. I took her ass like I owned it, in strong steady strokes, and on each downbeat pressed her clit solidly into the toy in my hand, and I felt her body start to tremble.

"Oh my *God*—Jack—this time—please—don't stop—I can't take it if you stop—"

"Never," I promised, taking her hard, grinding her into my hand with each thrust until she gasped like she'd been surprised.

"Jack—Jack! Oh!" she shouted, curling into the mattress and into my hand. She bucked beneath me with the force of her orgasm, and I had to follow her. I sped my thrusts up, and she arched back to give me more of her ass and that was it, her offering her ass to me, because she wanted me to take it, she wanted all my load—just like I'd always dreamed—

I came with a shout, my whole body lurching forward with the force of my orgasm as I planted my cock inside of her to take it from me. My hips twitched spasmodically against hers, my thrusting mindless, as I could feel my balls lifting and pumping as she drained them again.

I collapsed on top of her, feeling her breathing raggedly beneath me, until I rolled over, my cock sliding out of her to drape against my thigh. "I have never, ever, had sex this good."

She laughed melodiously, rolling onto her side. "You should never tell a woman that."

"Why?" I asked in all innocence.

"Because then she knows," she said and gave me a mysterious smile before snuggling up against me. I didn't press the matter, and not long after that we were asleep again.

CHAPTER FOUR
JACK

There was pizza, there were naps, there were movies, and there was snuggling, and anything else we could do short of needing condoms we did—she reached over and jacked me off because she could, and I loved the hot feel of her skin on mine, and the way my cum looked against her hand. And then I took one of those rubber sword-looking things out and fucked her while she played with herself, just to watch her come, to hear her voice rise and watch her body shake.

But at ten p.m. Thea looked at the clock on her phone, every bit a Cinderella. "I'm sorry Jack, but—"

"I know," I said softly. I'd looked at my phone an hour ago, and had been feeling the minutes count down since.

She rolled out of bed and stood. "This has been really amazing. But I've got to shower and—"

"I'll call a ride."

"Good," she said, and gave me an apologetic smile.

For all the fucking we'd done, there was a distance between us now—almost the same as the distance between us in high school.

She had her place, here, and I had mine, back in Texas. The past sixteen hours belonged to an alternate reality.

"Like, really amazing," she said, with emphasis, and then danced over to me to lean up and peck my cheek with a chaste kiss.

"Agreed," I said with a rueful smile, watching her walk through her bathroom door. She didn't even bother to close it as she stepped into her shower. Between the steam and the door's crinkled safety glass she probably couldn't see me, but she knew that I was there.

"It's okay if you have to pee, just don't flush!" she shouted, from the other side of the shower.

Her bathroom counter was laced with feminine things, perfumes and potions, and her make-up kit was like an arsenal, with just as many colors as I had at my tattoo station back home. I lifted a necklace out of a heart shaped bowl—it was a fat emerald encircled by diamonds.

Somewhere there was an admirer who could give her that. *How on earth could I compare?*

I couldn't.

That's why I had to go.

My stomach and my heart sank, as I watched her blurry body moving behind the shower door, rinsing me away, and I couldn't stand it.

If you'd asked me before that moment if I had had a possessive bone in my body, I would have said no—but watching her, I became a creature made of claws, and all I wanted was to grab hold of her and never let her go.

I slid the shower door open and stepped in.

"Jack!" she protested, as cold air swirled in with me. She was soaking wet, rivulets of water streaming down her face, her hair in wet blonde tassels—and she looked just like the girl I'd rescued from her shattered car. I put my hand out to touch her cheek and stroked my thumb across the small scar she had from the accident, right above her cheekbone. Without thinking, she leaned into it, like a cat.

"Are you clean yet?" I asked her.

Her eyes flashed up at me. "Not hardly."

"Then hand me the soap."

I rolled the soap between my hands until they were full of lather, and then soaped up every beautiful piece of her, washing all evidence of me away. She stood there and let me, like she knew I was trying to memorize her because I was, then I commanded: "Turn around."

She did as she was told, quivering, waiting—as I knelt down behind her and spread her ass wide. I pressed my tongue against her asshole and felt her whole body shake, as she instantly went up on her toes to give me access.

"Oh God, Jack." One of her hands darted up to grab the shower nozzle and bring it down, to run the water over her clit as I gently kissed her there, and then pushed my tongue inside.

Within seconds, she was moaning, begging, one hand pressed against the shower wall, the other holding the nozzle as she bent over. "Please, please," she danced for me, for her orgasm, in the spraying water as my tongue probed her. "Please."

I grabbed hold of her ass with both hands, loving the curve of it, the meat of it, the way kissing her here made her mine.

"Oh God, oh God," she started begging the Creator, and then, "Jack—Jack—Jack!" She named each wave of her orgasm after me, coming fast and hard, I saw it rippling through her body. She sagged against the wall to pant, as I pulled back.

"There," I said. There was no part of her now I had not known and tasted. No mysteries left. I stood, breathing in the thick steam. My cock was hard, curving up toward my belly, but it didn't matter —I was going to have a hard on for Thea until the day that I died. I took the shower head and ran it over myself, once, twice, and then got out of the shower to start raking myself with a towel. She stayed in the shower behind me, and I heard her phone beep as a message came in while I went to collect my clothing off of her floor.

Three minutes later, when my jeans were on and I was pulling on my shirt, she ran into her living room, phone in hand. "Don't go."

My hands paused in disbelief. "What?"

"You heard me," she said, licking her lips to smile. "How much longer are you in town for?"

"My flight leaves at three, tomorrow." I could feel my pulse at all points in my body, throbbing with hope.

"Change it. Go get your bags and come back. Give me another day here. We won't even leave the apartment. I'll bring home more condoms—a box."

The way she was looking at me—and the way I needed her, I'd always needed her—I answered before thinking about Bruce, or flights, or clients. "Bring home two."

I DID FLY HOME the day after that though, my cock chafed, my body sore. A hundred dollars to change the flight had bought me another day's time with her. When I got back to Dallas, Bruce only had one question.

"Was it worth it?"

"Completely."

"Good," he said with a laugh and then we went back to all business.

I HONESTLY DIDN'T EXPECT to hear from Thea again. We'd exchanged numbers, but both of us knew how impossible a relationship would be, so I didn't reach out to her. I didn't want to seem desperate, or worse yet, in denial.

So I was surprised when three days later, she sent me a text.

You still jerking off to me?

I smiled down at the phone while I considered what to type. *Every night.*

Good.

After that it was a week of silence then another tease and I couldn't resist responding. I knew all the things girls did to guys to yank their chains—and vice versa—and yet I still let her pull.

I tried to throw myself into my work, trying to not let her silences torment me—I had more than enough imagination to get by alone at night—and I had a lot of options, I appealed to a lot of types: girls my age who were every bit as tattooed as I was, older women looking to get into younger trouble, and church girls with a secret devil-may-care side. I'd had them all, and could get them again, but they all paled in comparison to Thea, my dancing Dorothy, who'd taken her ruby-red stilettos and pierced my heart.

I got her next text while I was in line at the grocery store. *I have two days off. Come out?*

Self-respecting Jack—the Jack I'd become since leaving my one-horse hometown—knew better than to respond. But high school Jack wagged his tail to agree.

AND SO FOR a while it was like that—her sending texts, me scrambling to buy flights and rebook appointments, ignoring when angry clients then cancelled on me. I didn't have any other obligations, other than to Bruce, who'd started to radiate a sense of weary disapproval.

My plane would land and I'd catch a cab or she'd pick me up, and we'd go straight to her apartment. I didn't ask why we never left it, or why she wouldn't let me. It didn't matter. I didn't want to know what the rest of Vegas held—it was a happy blur of neon until I reached the soft cotton of her sheets, the softer skin between her thighs.

Eight months passed like that, with me coming out and pounding her senseless every third or fourth week: Thea's hands clawing my back, my breath on her neck, both of us fucking like we were desperate, like the fucking was our air. Each time leaving her was a little harder, a little heavier, like my cock was setting an anchor into her that I buried deeper with every thrust.

And in between we'd lay beside one another, her shoulder tucked into my armpit, her head leaning in beneath my chin, and talk. I'd tell her about the tattoo studio I'd own someday, my own or Bruce's, if he left it to me when he retired like he was always threatening to. And she'd tell me about a trip she was saving for, she had it planned out, city by city, a literal trip around the world—not just in hostels, scraping by, but in style, at four star resorts wearing designer clothes, sitting by pools and going to galleries. It was what she was saving all her tips for, while other girls spent theirs on diapers or on drugs.

But sometimes late at night she'd seem sad. Our first nights together were always wild, and often as not we wouldn't make it to the bedroom, I'd end up taking her against her couch or on her floor. The nights after that though, I'd catch her staring into space and she'd feel distant, even though my arms were wrapped around her tight. When I'd ask her what was wrong, I could always sense the answer hiding right behind her teeth—but then she'd laugh and play it off with a 'nothing!'. And after that she'd rise up and devour me and her distractions worked—I couldn't ask her any more questions when her tongue was in my mouth.

I always wanted to push her away and find out more, but I was afraid I wouldn't like the answer. And I liked the sensation of her needing me, even if it was needing to distract me—or then having me distract her—which I was worried made me some sort of emotionally damaged sick-fuck...but not enough to stop flying out.

OVER THAT TIME, her collection of jewelry grew. I asked her about it in her bathroom one night, after she'd blown me in the shower, pulling back to let me shoot myself all over her perfect breasts.

She smiled disingenuously and laughed. "Oh, don't worry about that—it's all fake."

I doubted fake jewelry felt so solid or was engraved with the word 'Cartier'. But the things I wanted to say to her, the ways that I felt—I knew I had to keep them to myself. I didn't deserve her, I never had. All of this was glamour and luck, and if I breathed on it wrong the bubble would burst. Just like that first night when I'd seen her spinning, when my eyes had glinted off of her because she was too bright—I knew asking what this was now, if we were anything to each other, would break it.

Somehow I managed to be okay with that, always holding my hopes in reserve, trusting in the way she made me feel, in the way I knew I made her feel—until the day I landed and she didn't come to get me.

CHAPTER FIVE

JACK

I stood outside the terminal at ten PM, the desert heat radiating up from the ground, looking at my phone's rapidly dwindling battery, waiting for a text. I'd already sent her several and gotten zero response. After fifteen minutes and no Thea, I summoned an Uber and went to her apartment.

The door was shut and locked, but her car was in the parking lot.

"Thea?" I knocked politely at first, then harder, walking around to rap on her window with a worried fist. "Thea, are you okay?"

Nothing.

I didn't know what else to do. Call 911? Have them break into the apartment of the girl that I was part-time fucking? The girl who always looked like she was about to say she loved me, but never quite managed the words?

"Goddammit, Thea!" I pounded on her door with an open hand. When a neighbor's light came on, I sank back into the shadows. If she wasn't here, where else could she be? Or who else might know?

I ran down the cement stairs and called another car.

I HADN'T BEEN OUTSIDE of Vermillion in almost nine months, since the night Bruce and I'd first come there. I knew Thea danced—sometimes she had shifts when I visited—but I didn't let it bother me. When I was in town she came home to me every night, even if that wasn't until 4 or 5 AM. With my bag still on my shoulder, I pushed through the glass door.

The music was just as loud and the lights as dim as I remembered. It was a slow Tuesday night and girls swarmed me in hope.

"Hey," I asked the nearest one, leaning over to be heard. "Where's Thea?"

She made a face. "Thea?"

"Ruby," I remembered, her stage name a not-so-clever joke.

"Oh!" She brightened in recognition. "You don't want her. Not tonight," she said, trying to draw me further in.

"Yeah, I do," I said, fighting her for my arm. She relinquished it with a pout.

"Fine. She's in the back. But she's *busy*."

"Yeah?" Maybe she'd forgotten my flight, gotten the days mixed up—maybe she'd just gotten trapped here at the office.

She walked her fingers down my chest. "Yeah. So come back to me later," she said. "You're cute."

"Thanks," I said, and sidled through the room to the back, where the same Samoan bouncer blocked my path.

"Closed tonight. Private party," he explained.

"I get that, but—is Thea, I mean Ruby, okay?"

"She's fine."

"I just want to see her," I leaned forward.

"No, you don't."

But it was too late. I'd caught a glimpse of her beyond his broad shoulders as he moved ever so slightly to the side, at the center stage in the room with all the alcoves, twirling sadly around a pole, with a group of men shouting on. My time in high school and my time on the streets had given me a sixth sense about the moods of crowds—there was tension in there. Something was wrong.

"She's not safe—"

"Neither are you," the Samoan said. But when I went to push past him, he gave way, content to let me make my own mistakes.

Thea stopped, mid-swing, grabbing the pole and lowering herself to the ground, looking terrified as a monstrously sized man in a crisp suit behind her stood up.

"I knew you'd show up."

He was shouting and I still had to practically read his lips over the music. But he was holding her phone—and I realized it was one of his necklaces dangling from her throat.

All this time I thought there'd been some fool buying jewelry for her—instead of realizing I was some fool buying plane tickets.

"Is this the guy you've been texting behind my back?" he shook her phone at her, before flinging it to the ground to shatter.

Thea sobbed fresh tears, smearing her mascara, but not enough to cover what looked like a black-eye.

"Did you hurt her?" I shouted, stalking forward. There were five other men there, and two went for holsters in their waistbands.

"He's no one. He's not anything," I heard her say. I knew what she was doing and why she was saying it, but her words still felt like slaps.

"I think he disagrees." The man in the suit smiled at me, his teeth glittering as whitely as the diamonds at her throat. "She's mine," he growled, over the music's omnipresent bass. "Turn around now and I'll let you walk away. Don't, and you'll be lucky to crawl."

"Go!" Thea shouted at me, pleading. "Just go!"

But going would mean leaving her there, with them. And I realized what my heart, soul, and cock had been telling me all along—I was done with leaving Thea behind.

I looked at the men. I didn't think they'd actually start shooting in a private establishment. And me? I'd spent enough time getting beat to get good at giving beatings back.

"Fuck you," I said, dropping my bag.

The nearest man lunged up toward me, begging for a fight,

hoping to make a quick show of things for his boss—but he'd had too much to drink, or was lazy and out of practice—he came high and I went low, punching him solidly in his gut, knocking the wind out of him and dancing aside, looking for the next contestant.

He arrived on cue and feigned a headshot, before aiming for my ribcage. I spun away from him and pulled back, noticing another trying to circle in from behind. All of these guys had grease in their hair, like some pomade-based mob—I backed up and grabbed hold of a chair to swing it at the nearest man like a frustrated lion tamer. It spun him back and I sagged forward after it with the force of my swing, then heard Thea shout: "Jack!"

Another guy lunged in and clocked my jaw. Only experience with having been hit before saved me—I went with the motion just enough to escape getting concussed—and I reeled down, coming up just as hard, inside his defenses with an upper-cut, as another man came in from behind to punch my kidneys.

The man in the suit ignored all this, grabbing Thea's waist, hauling her away like he was King Kong. "No!" she shouted, pounding at him, unable to get traction to resist with her heels.

I turned to see this, leaving my back exposed. The Samoan guy stepped aside to let them through like this sort of thing happened all the time and I shouted as someone cracked the back of my skull. I ignored the blinding pain from this, running after her shouting, "Thea!" and tumbled into the next room due to the weight of the guys coming after me from behind—together all of us set the Samoan off balance.

The music in the real club was even louder—but the girls on stage, doing some sort of duo act, stopped to gasp. I felt another blow land as Thea was dragged into the shadows. "Thea!" I shouted, as someone hit my chest.

That was it. I whirled and I fought like a cornered animal. Eyes, ears, groins, kneecaps—I wanted to make a mess. A man grunted then howled, clutching his face as he stumbled blind, another staggered to one side, as his leg suddenly went soft. There were screams from behind us, girls, patrons—until the music came to a halt. There was a three second gap where the only sound was fists hitting flesh, and then the lights pointed away from the stage, blinding everyone at once.

"This is my club." Rosalie, Thea's boss, strode out on stage in a golden evening gown, her voice booming over the newly hushed crowd. "And you all will behave. *Look at me.*"

I wanted to save Thea—but couldn't look away from her, even as I wanted to—I tried! And as she scanned the audience, I knew she knew it—that none of us could—or the suited man's thugs would still be beating on me. Instead, the one whose eye I'd nearly taken out stood beside me, a hand clutched to his face to cup blood while he watched her with his remaining good one.

Rosalie started to sway as a piano came on—I was surprised when I recognized, 'Put a Little Sugar in my Bowl'—and she smiled indulgently as Nina Simone started to sing, reaching behind her back to unfasten something.

She walked to the end of the stage—slinking was a better way to describe it—moving fluidly, like she had fewer bones than the rest of us, and two lights followed her. Then, when she got there, she lifted her arms overhead, all the better to let her dress shine, it made her look like a living flame. She rocked her chest and hips in time to the music, making her dress fall, inch by inch, revealing luminously dark skin. As Nina crooned about needing sugar, Rosalie mesmerized us all—I could barely remember why I'd come in to Vermillion, and my fears for Thea dimmed. Rosalie was the only woman here worth looking at tonight—and I wanted to see all of her.

The dress fell from the edge of her soft breasts, exposing nipples slightly darker than the surrounding skin, with wide areolas, like the eyes on a butterfly's wings, and all the blood in my body sunk low.

Thea.

Thea in the arms of some stranger. A maniac.

I wanted to leave, I had to leave—but as often as I told my feet to move, my eyes to look away, and my cock *no!*, all of me was ensor-celled by Rosalie.

"That's good, isn't it?" she whispered. The dress had taken a dramatic fall off of her hips, and she'd stepped out of it to move freely. "Now," she said, and even though the music had stopped and faded, she still danced hypnotically, undulating like the ocean under moonlight. "Ladies, tonight is over. Take your tips and go home. Forget what you saw here, and come back next shift. That includes you, George."

I'd forgotten some of them were still in the room. I heard the sound of women following her commands, shuffling to pick up the wads of cash they'd dropped in the confusion, walking deliberately towards the back. A man tumbled out of the DJ booth to follow them.

"The rest of you men—your night is also over. Forget what you saw here. Forget why you hurt. Go home, remember nothing, and never return," she said, and I could feel her words clouding my mind, trying to make me obey.

Thea! Part of my soul kept screaming.

"Except for you, Bobbie," Rosalie said, changing her mind on the stage. "You come back as often as you want. Fantasia would be very sad without you, and I would be very sad without your cash."

A man closer to the stage than I was shouted, "Yeehaw!" and lifted his arms in triumph.

What the—*Thea*—where was—*Thea*—how did I—*Thea*—I stood still, fighting myself, as the men all around me trundled off like strange zombies, two of them helping the kneecapped third.

The Samoan walked up to the stage pulling earplugs out and offered Rosalie a hand which she took, letting me see the lighter shade of her sex as she stepped down.

Thea!

"Now that that's done," I heard her say to him as I fought not to move. To move was to give in and if I gave in what was next?

Rosalie walked over to me, unabashed in her nakedness, with the Samoan close behind.

"You want me to?" the Samoan asked, offering violence as he raised a meaty hand high.

She pondered me for a moment. "No. But stay near." Then she took my jaw, sore from where it'd gotten cold-cocked and twisted my head so that I was looking directly at her. "You. *Follow me.*"

This command there was no disobeying. As she turned, I followed without choice.

CHAPTER SIX
JACK

W e went through the back room, past the spatters of blood on the ground, the tumbled furniture, someone else's tooth, and into backstage. It was like going into a different world—it smelled like fruits and candies, and a mist of Aqua-net might've permanently been in the air. Vanity mirrors were surrounded by bright lights, some of them flickering, and the edges of the mirrors held feather boas and fresh thongs.

Thea—my mind begged me, urging me to remember, to get to wherever she'd been taken to.

Rosalie led me through one more doorway and I realized we were inside her private room. She had her own mirror and make-up, and the rest of the room held a couch, two plush chairs, and an over-stuffed closet where clothes covered in sequins strained to get out. She closed the door behind us and pulled a white satin robe off a hook and on. And when she was done she turned to survey me.

"You are a good fighter—but a stupid man." She lifted a casual hand and snapped her fingers. "There. Now you're you. What's your name?"

I blinked, feeling free for the first time since she'd started talking. "I have to go."

Her eyebrows rose. "Where?"

"I—I don't know. Wherever they took her. Do you know where?"

"Yes." Her head tilted and she gave me a smug smile. "But—you and what army, as they say?" Her French accent was amused. "Do you have friends? Ones willing to die for you and your stripper?"

"Girlfriend," I corrected, in case that'd make her more inclined to help me.

"*Really*," she said, with a snide tone of disbelief.

"We've been seeing each other."

She tsked. "I hate to tell you, lover-boy, but she's been seeing a lot of people. It may come as a surprise, but your dearest darling is an attention whore."

Rosalie had just confirmed all my deepest fears—that while Thea was precious to me, I was not special to her, and yet…. "That doesn't make him hitting her right."

She rocked back slightly, eyes half-lidded in concentration. "True. But your noble heart doesn't change the odds. Still though, you must really love her, if you can remember her after my show." She walked around me in a circle, tracing a hand over my arm, my chest, my back.

"What was that tonight? What did you do to us?"

"Just a trick. There's a hundred hypnotists on the Strip that could do the same, easily."

She sounded dismissive—and I knew she was lying. I knew how I'd felt, how hard I'd had to hold on to Thea's memory. But now that I was free of her 'tricks' I needed to do something quickly. "Are you going to help me? Or not?"

"Yes," she said, returning to stand in front of me. "But only because you may be of some use."

I had no idea what I could possibly do to help some stripper hypno-queen, but it didn't matter. "Good. Tell me who took her and where, so I can tell the police."

"Oh?" she said, then burst out laughing. "You are a charming fool! The men she's with—they either own the cops—or the few good ones are waiting for a big enough bust to make rocking the boat worthwhile. I regret to tell you that none of them are going to go out of their way to help your precious Ruby."

"Thea."

"Thea," she corrected, with a smirk.

I waited, eyes scanning the room. Was the bouncer out there getting back-up? Making calls to someone who had guns? "Then— how can you help me?" Whatever it was, we needed to start doing it fast. "Tell me where—"

"You really do love her?" she interrupted. Her hands fell to her robe's sash, and she started circling me again, like a shark.

"I do." I wish I'd told Thea as much before all this—that I'd managed to be a stronger man, and risk rejection to gain the truth.

One of her eyebrows delicately arched. "And you're willing to do anything to save her? Anything I tell you to do?"

"As long as it saves her, I am." My intentions solidified. I'd rescued Thea once, I would rescue her again.

"And you mean that?" she purred. "No matter what needs to be done?"

I nodded, at first slow, and then more strongly. I knew I was sealing a pact of some sort, but at the end of it was *Thea*.

At that, Rosalie untied her robe's sash, and I heard the soft *whoosh* of fabric as her robe fell to the ground, leaving her naked again. I blinked. "What're you—"

"Shh," she hushed me. "Be *quiet*, and *behave*," she commanded, compelling me anew. "If you want to save her as badly as you say you do, you're going to have to do it my way."

I did what I was told and swallowed.

She paced forward and eyed me again, as if measuring me, and then pulled me toward her wide velvet couch. She sat down first, spreading her legs wide. I looked away and she laughed. "A prude? No. That won't do," she said with a laugh, then gestured. Come *here*," she commanded. "*Turn around, and sit down,*" she said, while patting the space between her thighs.

I did as I was told instantly, without thinking. She wrapped herself around me, encircling me with her dark legs as I felt her breasts press against my back. "You smell nice," she whispered to herself, breathing me in.

How was this helping Thea, who even now was off with some monster? I tried to strain, to free myself to ask, but there was no breaking free.

Rosalie played her hands up and down my chest, feeling the muscles my shirt barely hid, then tugged it up out of my belt to touch skin. She made an appreciative sound. "So strong. You'll make such a good plaything, I can tell. I might even keep you for myself, for a time."

My shirt rose higher, until I could feel her skin against mine and after that she gasped.

"Look at you!" She climbed higher so that she could see my chest. "A magic man!" Her hands inspected my tattoos, pushing me forward, pulling me back, until she'd seen and touched them all. "I'm magic too, you know. If you're lucky, I will show you."

Thea!

She breathed me in again, lips grazing against my neck, one hand in my hair. She arched her hips forward, grinding herself against me. "Yes. This is right," she said, but I had no such surety. *What the fuck was going on? Why couldn't I get free?* I closed my eyes and tried to concentrate on what I knew was true. *Thea. Thea. Thea.*

"You never did tell me your name," Rosalie said. "*Speak it,*" she commanded.

"Jack," I answered.

She laughed to herself. "How fitting." And her hands reached around me to undo my belt buckle as she kissed my back. When the buckle was undone, she went for the button-fly of my jeans, opening them one by one, reaching inside blindly to find my cock.

"*Get hard*, Jack," she whispered in my ear as her hand wrapped me.

My blood sank. I didn't want to—this was a waste of time! I needed to go, to rescue Thea—but I couldn't move an inch off of her couch. All I could do was look down and see her hand against me, the contrast between our skin colors striking.

"I want you *harder* than you've ever been," she whispered, and my body betrayed me. "Oh—that's nice," she said as my girth became more solid. "Someday—oh how I will use that cock."

Her breath on my neck was warm, and she continued to kiss me, my ear, my jaw, my collarbone, as her grinding behind me began anew. I could feel the folds of her pussy rubbing against me, the rhythmic way she pulsed against my back, using me to pleasure herself.

Thea!

And then her hand started slowly stroking.

I didn't want to respond—*I needed to go! Where was Thea and what was happening to her?*—but there was no way not to—it was like my cock was a separate entity, a traitor to the rest of me, a monster wanting to be fed. My breath caught and quickened, and at that she purred.

"See? Your body knows what it wants. Just as mine does." She reached between us with her free hand and separated herself from me for a moment, then started stroking my back in arcane patterns, streaking it with wetness gleaned from her pussy. "When this is over Jack, you might have saved Thea, but you will be mine. I will snap and you will come. I'll say fuck and you'll ask who."

Her hand's rhythm sped up around my shaft. "How many times did you push this cock in and out of her? You're mad at me now—but I'm giving you a lifetime of pussy, Jack. All the pussy in the world."

Her hips bobbed against my back as her mouth bit at my ear. *Where was Thea, and what was happening to me?* Rosalie's expert hand knew just how long to make each stroke, how fast to go, how much pressure to apply. The need to come rose up inside, unbidden.

"Not yet," she said, stopping her hand and pinching my tip. Her hips stroked hard against me, the muscles of her legs pulling her close and then pushing her back again. I could feel broad swathes of her wetness as her pussy anointed me. "Oh, magic man," she purred, sliding on and off. "Soon all your magic will be mine." Her voice was breathy, soft, and the way she rocked into me more firmly, pressing harder, longer, making her grinding contact more rough. "Oh yes—ohhhh," she moaned, rocking back into the couch, letting go of me entirely. "Yes, yes, yes," she said, with three hard strokes down.

I could feel her shuddering behind me, her legs quivering in the nest they'd made around me. And the next sound she made was an indulgent one. "See?" she said, leaning forward, bringing her hand back around to touch my cock.

The hand she stroked me with was wet now, from herself. The extra lubrication made her hand feel like a pussy and—*Thea—oh Thea—*

Rosalie covered me with her body once again, her chin digging against my neck. "You're so close, aren't you?"

And as she said it, I was. All I could do was pant and nod.

"Do you want to come inside my hand?" she asked, licking the shell of my ear. My hips thrust in helpless answer, and she laughed. "You would do anything to save her, wouldn't you."

It wasn't even a question. It didn't need to be. "*Anything,*" I managed to growl through gritted teeth.

"So willful! So strong!" She seemed pleased, her breath hot against my neck. "Good. Because after this...there will be no turning back." She started stroking me in earnest, then reached around to push two fingers into my mouth. They tasted like her, and she used them like a fish-hook to twist my head down and away from her, exposing my neck to her mouth. "Give me your cum, Jack. I want to feel the heat of it, I want to watch you spurt, when you can no longer stop yourself."

I began to have an inkling of the devil's pact I'd signed. Nothing here was right or sane. Rosalie was up in my head somehow, and I couldn't get her out. It scared me, but I also couldn't help but obey.

"That's right," she said, licking a line up my neck. "You're so strong, Jack. But no man is stronger than I am," she whispered. "*Come for me.*"

My body listened. My hips thrust forward into her hand and then I came like a volcano, cum geysering as she kept stroking it out of me. I thrashed against her, unable to groan but still needing to express the awesome horror of what she'd done.

I watched her bring one hand full of my cum up to her mouth and saw her lick her palm roughly out of the corner of my eye, my head still twisted by her fingers and heard her say, "Fluids seal a pact."

Then teeth grew, fangs like a snake's, which made sense because that was clearly what she was, some sort of slithering demon, and she plunged them into my neck. I wanted to scream but couldn't, trapped by her earlier command, but I could spasm in surprise, the end of my orgasm changing into something terrified. Her fangs ground into me, tearing muscle, hitting bone, as they ripped into my flesh, and I felt the heat of my own blood running down my chest.

I was dying here—without Thea.

Rosalie reared up, her mouth bloody—*with my blood!*—fangs still out, looking triumphant.

"*Bite*, my foolish child," she said, and I bit down on her fingers in my mouth just like she'd told me too.

My teeth pierced her skin and her blood, sweet and tangy, poured out of them, filling my mouth—I let it slosh out of my lips in horror.

"*Swallow*," she commanded, and I did—I had too—and felt a thick mouthful slide back and down, landing in my stomach like a lead weight. My stomach burbled against it—I was instantly sure it was poisoning me.

"Good," she said, her eyes glittering. "Very good, Jack." She pulled her hand out of my mouth and somehow it was whole.

Released from her spell, I raised a frightened hand and felt streaks of my clotting blood against my cotton shirt, but found my neck itself intact. She leaned back on the couch behind me, reaching out to stroke my hair. "It's a rare gift that I've given you, Jack. You should feel very special."

I didn't—maybe her ability to coerce me to do things was fading. Suddenly my vision started to go dark. "What's happening to me?" I asked. I started to panic, even more so than I had been.

She kept stroking my hair. "Don't worry, it's normal. You'll be out for three days while you change. I'll protect you, of course. I might even see fit to use you some between now and then. Too bad you won't remember."

I tried to say something else, but my throat closed. Acid rose in my stomach and my limbs were going numb. The world shrank in on itself, and I could almost feel my mind slow.

I already knew I'd made an epically bad decision, and as everything went black I only had time for one last thought.

Thea—what have I done?

CHAPTER SEVEN

ANGELA

"Come on, Angie—I just need you to come with me tonight."
I loved Willa Heartwood to death, but it was already that clear this would be the worst decision she'd ever talked me into.

We were in my bedroom upstairs, just a week before school was starting. Willa was going to Luna community college to figure out what she wanted to be, whereas I was going to UNLV as an art major. High school had made it abundantly clear that painting and drawing were the only things I was good at—but I was really, *really* good at them.

"You won't even have to stay long," she wheedled. "Just be my wing-woman. Help me get in the door."

"Who is this guy? Have I met him?"

"No. Remember a week ago when you ditched me?"

"Because my parents wanted me to hang out with them." Code words for: *'You're spending too much time with Willa again, and we don't want her crazy to stick.'*

"Well, I went to that club downtown and hung out, out back, trying to meet the band. There were these guys there and—oh my God, you should've seen him." Willa's eyes were intent on mine. "He was beautiful. He was amazing." Willa didn't go boy-crazy for just anyone, so hearing her be so enthused was quite unlike her.

"And...you talked to him?" I asked.

"No. He was so pretty I didn't have the guts. But after he rode off —*on a motorcycle*," she emphasized, as though that were the important part, "this older chick came over and told me about him. Said his girlfriend had just broken up with him and where he'd be tonight."

"And why isn't she humping him herself, if he's so hot?"

"Because she was with another guy there." Willa leaned in. "I think they're like in a gang."

"Willa!" I stared at her. "You're kidding, right?"

"I absolutely am not. I wouldn't ask you if it weren't important to me, Angie, but I've spent the entire last week thinking about him." She threw herself across my bed, arms wide. "You would understand, if you'd been there."

I flopped down on the bed beside her. "Probably."

Willa and I had been best friends since elementary school In Las Vegas, where people moved in and out like a perpetual tide, this was an accomplishment. There was nothing about me she didn't know— what boy bands members I'd had crushes on and in what order, which boys in high school I'd liked. She'd been the one to hand me a pad under the stall when my period had started, and had been the person I'd hung out and watched Netflix with when we skipped proms—both of them.

And I, in turn, knew everything about her. Why she hung out at my house so much—to hide out from her angry dad—and helped her cheat on algebra in 8th grade enough to pass. I remembered the first time she'd smoked pot and the first time she'd gotten me some. And I'd been the one she called half an hour after she'd lost her virginity, more interested in telling me about it than in hanging out with the boy who'd done the deed.

She was the wild-one, I was straight-laced. I kept her safe and she kept things fun. We'd spent practically our whole lives together, joined at the hip, just like we were now on my bed. But school was looming and we'd be going to vastly different places. We'd been talking a big game about moving out of our parent's houses and moving in together, but we hadn't gotten our acts together yet. Maybe it wouldn't happen at all. Maybe this was the beginning of the end.

She bounced up on an elbow, her thoughts running opposite of mine. "You still haven't answered, Ang."

Her dark curls fanned out around her face as she grinned, hopeful I'd come along on one last adventure. And if she was there—how could I not? "Sure. Fine," I grinned back at her.

"Yes!" She leapt off my bed and ran for my closet.

I LET her dress me up in short shorts and a tank, and we raced out of the house together before my parents could see. Then she drove us out to a strip mall in the middle of nowhere, where a dive bar faced a line of bikes. We got out of the car, but when she started walking toward them I stopped. "This is where we're going?"

"I know," she said, apologizing. "I drove by earlier this week and didn't have the guts to go in. I couldn't be doing this without you."

"We shouldn't be doing this at all," I complained.

"We just go inside, and see if he's there. If he's not then we wait a little bit and we leave, okay? That's it. Nothing major."

"Willa," I complained.

"Please. One last time." She wove her fingers through my own and tugged me toward the door.

That was the problem with my relationship with Willa. I had a hard time telling her no. "All right," I said, dragging my feet as she pulled me in to the bar.

Masculinity was in the air here—there weren't all that many other girls, just a lot of men, drinking hard, playing pool, and having heavy conversations.

The bartender—Davis, from the patch on his jacket—gave us both a wise look. "You girls don't belong here."

"I've been here before," Willa said, a bold-faced lie.

He gave her a once-over. "Maybe, maybe not. But her?" he said, looking at me. "I'd remember."

I hid behind my blonde hair, feeling both naked and gawky, wishing I was wearing a lot more clothes.

"Well she's with me," she said, looping her arm through mine. "We're staying. And we're both twenty-two."

"Uh-huh," he said. "And what're you drinking?'

"Beer?" I hazarded.

"Whiskey," Willa said, more sure of herself.

Davis worked the taps and handed us glasses bubbling with carbonation. "Diet Coke."

I looked to Willa, in case she'd gotten a better fake ID and was willing to push things. Instead though, she pulled out a ten and handed it over. "Thanks." He took it and didn't offer any change.

It was completely unlike Willa to let such rudeness slide. "You must really like this guy," I said, as we slunk off to the bar's far side.

"Trust me. He's worth it," she said, taking a sip from her glass.

"What if he's not here today? Maybe he has better things to do."

"I saw his bike out front," she said, giving me a sly wink.

A door pushed open from the back to pass a beer through and I could hear the sounds of laughter, men and more women's voices, and scent barbecued meat and cigars from a patio outside.

"And what if he's back there?" I wondered.

"Let's go see," she said, hopping off her stool.

I looked around the bar again, at the worrisomely huge guys keeping an eye on us. "Willa, no," I said, and meant it.

She opened her mouth to argue then came to her senses with a nod. "You're right." She got back on her barstool. "Let's just wait. If he comes in, it was meant to be."

"Yeah." I sipped on my Coke, wondering if I should hope to see him or not. Willa kept her eyes on the door, while I kept my eyes on her. I couldn't remember a time when I didn't want to practically be her. Being with her was the next best thing.

Just then the door swung open behind her, framing him in daylight. He was Nordic, clearly, maybe Scandinavian. His shoulders were almost as wide as the doorway and he was at least 6'4". And with his long hair and leather jacket, he looked like he'd come off the cover of a romance novel, the dirty kind we'd hid from our moms when we were fifteen. I felt my heart stop and an inconvenient throb from between my thighs.

Willa turned to face me as he went down the hall. "That was him. You see what I mean now?"

"Yeah," I breathed. But—I looked down the hall he'd walked down—to the bathrooms. We didn't have much time. "What's your amazing plan?"

She held up a hand and counted fingers down. As I heard a distant door squeak open, over the country on the jukebox, she reached one, and leaned in. "This," she whispered, her dark curls brushing my cheek, right before she kissed me.

I had only kissed three boys. Once in fifth grade, behind the jungle-gym, a bad idea all around. The second in seventh, at the bus-stop, on his last day at school before moving, the culmination of a year-long crush. And the third in tenth grade, outside the science hall, after which he'd written me a note explaining that he was in love with someone else. So my track record wasn't great, but I could've tried harder. There were boys who liked me, and I liked them—but I'd always been scared of what I'd do next. My mom always wanted me to be *good*, without ever quite defining what that was. All I ever knew was that if I ever let myself be with a boy, after the books I'd read and dreams I'd had, *good* was the precise opposite of what I'd be. Every time I thought too long about what I really *wanted*, it felt like a tornado was chewing me up inside. It made me worried that if I let even one part of what I hoped for out—how desperately wanted to get *f-u-c-k-e-d*, even though I'd never even let a boy hold me before—all of my lusts and urges and hopes would tear out, all at once, and destroy the countryside.

It seemed safer to keep that part of me tightly corked, like a genie in a bottle, where it couldn't hurt anyone—least of all me.

But then Willa was kissing me—and none of my books or dreams could've prepared me for that.

Her lips were soft and it felt natural to tilt my head to fit hers completely. Her tongue asked my lips for entrance, and I let it in, slowly opening up to this new experience. And then her hands were in my hair and I was leaning forward, using my tongue back and....

"Well what do we have here?" said a sonorous voice from beside us. Willa pulled back, staring at me, breathing hard—the same way I was breathing too. Then she looked up at him.

"We're just friends. Close friends," she said, and her hand slid up on my thigh. "I came here once before—I know Nikki—she said this was a fun place."

His eyes narrowed. "Yeah," he said. "I know Nikki too."

Willa dared a smile. "So, maybe we can go back to the real party with you?"

He looked from one to the other of us again and it was like his gaze was hot, making anywhere it touched me flush. I looked away, unable to meet his eyes. "Sure," he said, and Willa was off her barstool in a heartbeat, her hand finding mine to drag off on our next stage of this adventure. "Unless you two wanted to party with me, alone."

I dared to look up and saw him staring directly at me. Challenging me. If we went with him, I knew we wouldn't be able to turn back. But I also knew I wouldn't have to worry about frightening him with how secretly hungry I was, either.

"Ang?" Willa asked softly. I looked to her and saw her nod, then I was nodding too.

A wicked smile crept across his face. "Follow me," he said, and took us around the bar.

CHAPTER EIGHT
ANGELA

There was a room in back, his room, I gathered, paneled in wood with a large bed and desk. Willa and I stood, nervously holding hands as he set the latch of the door—more for privacy than imprisonment, I hoped. The sounds of the bar outside were all muted to a dull roar.

"You get used to that," he said, dismissing it. "I'm Gray. And you are?"

"Angela," I said.

"Willa," Willa responded, adding, "And she's a virgin."

I glared at her. "Thanks for ratting me out."

"I didn't want him to hurt you."

Gray stood and walked over to loom. "Are you really?" he asked, as I went red again.

"Yeah," I said with a nod.

"And you?" he asked Willa.

"Not so much anymore." I knew all about Willa's escapades with Boromir—his parents were huge Tolkien fans—in the back of 'Boringmir's' car, until they'd broken up because he was too dull to stand.

"Well," he said, giving us both an amused look. "Usually these things are more natural, and more liquor fueled, but I'll take the honesty of youth any day. Come here, my slightly wiser Willa," he said, leaning down.

He caught her head in his hands and I was forced to watch as he was kissing her mouth, the mouth I'd just tasted. Then he pulled up and looked at me. "How does that make you feel? Be honest."

And for the first time in my life I admitted there was a dark drive inside me. "Hungry."

He looked pleased at that. "For?"

I couldn't explain it. All I knew was that all my life I'd felt left out, in the pursuit of some hollow perfection, trying to be the person my mother, my teachers, my pastor wanted me to be, instead of what I was. "Everything," I answered truthfully.

He gave me a wicked grin. "Good," he said, his voice low, and went back to kissing her.

Willa made small appreciative noises and wrapped her arms around his neck, stroking her hands up into his hair. He pulled her body nearer, bending down, practically picking her up to make her fit him and she let him, curving her body against his like a snake. Watching them together, all the lonely parts of my body ached, wondering when we would finally get touched, when would it be our turn to finally let go. I reached up and pulled off my tank-top, throwing it aside, standing in my bra and shorts, hoping to draw him near.

My actions did not go unnoticed. Gray pulled up from her mouth and looked over at me, making a thoughtful sound and reached out for me as Willa made room. I stepped over, hesitantly. Willa wrapped an arm around my waist as I reached for hers—I was safe with her, as long as she was here, she wouldn't let anything bad happen to me —or at least anything bad would happen to us, together.

"Don't be frightened," Gray said, the corner of his lips lifting into a smirk. One of his hands went up into my hair and pulled my head back a little bit. He leaned forward and kissed, not my mouth, but my neck, from chin to earlobe—just like I could hear Willa doing to him on the other side.

I let go of her and ran my hands up his shoulders for balance, my fingers finding the leather of his vest slippery and cool. One of his hands ran roughly down my side, stopping at my hips, finding purchase in the waistband of my shorts to pull me near. I tilted my head, trying to find his mouth with mine—but he was kissing Willa instead—so I went for his neck, lips brushing against his golden stubble. He twisted his head back to meet mine and finally found my mouth with his. He was taller, stronger, and he knew what he wanted—his tongue pressed in, his lips spread mine, and it felt like I was being engulfed. His tongue painted the inside of my mouth, kissing me deeply, stroking in and out, mirroring what I so wanted to happen later—my imagination went into overdrive, and when he rose up, I swooned. He chuckled, easily holding me.

"Ditch these," he said, shaking my shorts. "And you—" he looked to Willa, who was already shucking off all her clothes.

I'd seen her in shared dressing rooms in the mall a thousand-thousand times. But I'd never seen her like this—*thought of her like this*—before. She was a little taller than I was, and intellectually I knew she was curvy and been appropriately jealous, but until now I'd never realized just how beautiful her curves could be. I reached out for her and she walked forward, letting me put a fluttering hand on the belly of her breast and to stroke her nipple with my thumb.

Gray made a low satisfied sound in his throat and turned toward her, going down almost to a kneel, to kiss her other breast. She gasped as his lips met her skin and then moaned, looking over his head at me with dark eyes, as I stepped in to kiss her over him.

One of her hands rose up to hold me to her mouth, the other to pull him in, and I caught her next moan and felt it thrill through me, as his hair stroked against my stomach. I felt a hand reach up behind me and set my bra free and him turn, shoving the fabric out of the way to kiss at my breast the way he had hers, and then the moans were mine.

This was—it was—finally happening to me. Not someone else. Not in a book or one of Willa's stories.

There was a man—a man, not a boy—kissing *me*.

I moaned softly as the stubble of his chin grazed my ribs and his tongue rolled over my nipple. Everything I'd ever done to it in the dark, in secret, could not compare. That, plus Willa's mouth, her soft lips pulling and pressing against my own, as our tongues matched one another—the low heat in my hips caught fire and started to burn. I reached for the waistband of my shorts and undid all buttons quickly—and felt Gray's hand helping me from the back to tug them off, and then cup my ass.

He rose between us suddenly, setting us apart, and began taking off layers of leather. His vest he put on the back of his desk chair, and Willa's hand found mine to hold, both of us content to watch him. His shirt came off next—and we could see the extraordinary muscles in his arms and back bunch and fold as he tugged the t-shirt he was wearing underneath overhead, revealing wolf-themed tattoos across his back, then he turned toward us. His chest was wide, his hips more narrow, and looking at the both of us, he hitched his thumbs into his belt.

I could see the outline of his hard-on through his jeans. Penises were mysterious things I'd only seen online. I knew what they were used for—and I wanted him to *use* me—but....

Gray's eyes followed my expression and reached down, undoing his belt buckle. Willa's hand squeezed mine and then let go, running over to him to help. He smiled at her eagerness, and I watched as she pulled his penis out, stroking it with her hand.

"You really never have seen one of these before?" he said, looking over at me, amusedly. Willa was going down to her knees in front of him.

I shook my head. Willa started lapping at it with her tongue. Was that what you did in real life, not just porn? He made another low sound, stroking through her hair with one hand, and with the other, grabbed the base of his penis, before looking directly at me. "This is my cock, girl. And I'm going to fuck you so well with it that I ruin you for all other men."

I stood there, transfixed, equal parts scared and delighted and everything else, so I said the only thing I could think of: "Prove it to me."

His smile stretched wolfishly, showing a row of even white teeth. "I will."

Then he closed his eyes and leaned his head back, letting his jaw drop a little, under Willa's ministrations. I came closer, close enough to watch her mouth take him in. She looked up and gave me a mischievous wink.

He, while extraordinarily hot and lust inducingly cocky, needed to be put in his place. So I knelt down beside her, and the next time she pulled her head off his cock—a word I liked vastly better than penis—I caught her mouth with mine, instead. My hands ran up her body, to touch both her breasts. They were so perfect, I wanted to feel them forever—I wanted to feel all her soft places, one by one. His cock bobbed nearby, and Willa stroked it with one hand, as I started stroking lower on her.

Gray laughed then reached down. With strength I didn't know a man could possess, he grabbed us both up and tossed us on his bed. We bounced apart, but found each other quickly again, mouth to mouth, chest to chest. Her leg slid between mine and I naturally started to grind on it—and behind her, I could see Gray removing the rest of his clothes.

When he was naked, I thought he'd join us, but instead he stretched out alongside us, watching us touch one another like a cat watched prey. I was curious about him and all his promises—but Willa's mouth was on my nipple and one of her hands was reaching inside my panties and I needed to know where it would go—then his hand reached in, pulling her chin up and away from me, back to him. He kissed her as her hand stroked lower and my mouth found her breast and her other hand found his cock and—he pulled it away to pull a condom on.

Oh God. We were really doing this.

My legs squeezed together in excited fear just as Willa tried to push a finger inside. Instead her fingers found my spot, the one romance novels had guided me toward in tenth grade, where I knew to rub until my body roared—I trembled at her hand there, and at the thought of finally making my fever dreams come true.

"Come here, Willa," Gray said, pulling her away from me bodily. She went, willing, as he rolled her on her back and moved himself to lay above her, supported on his arms, and then looked at me. "Princess, I want you to watch," he said, reaching out one hand to catch my chin. "Everything I do to her, I'm going to do to you, and then some. Only I'm going to wait until you're begging me."

"Can—I—help?" I stuttered the words.

He gave me another easy smile. "I'd be disappointed if you didn't." Then he lowered his head to kiss her, leaving his body arched up, condomed cock jutting between them. Willa made more small loving sounds as she was screened off by his hair, and I was forced to imagine what was going through her mind. I felt the bed move as I saw her hips rise, asking him for entry, and watched him release his own clenched ass and tight thighs as he lowered himself to take her.

"Willa," I gasped, grabbing her hand with my own. She took it and held it back just as tight as he started to push and she started to moan. My other hand went between my legs to touch myself, I couldn't help it, I didn't know what else to do.

Gray leaned up from her and gazed at me as he gave her steady strokes. Willa's lips parted with a pant, her head back, her perfect breasts falling slightly to each side. I leaned in to kiss her as each move he made rocked the bed. She brought her hands up to grab my hair and kiss me fiercely. "I love you, Angie," she whispered in my ear.

"I know," I whispered back. I could feel him moving her, it was almost as good as him moving me—he reached over and grabbed my ass, holding it tight, then looked at my trapped hand.

"You know how to touch yourself? Good," he said, his voice low.

"Touch yourself for me. I want you so wet for me," he said, still rhythmically stroking into my best friend. The cognitive dissonance was harsh until it broke me, and then everything made sense. I'd always loved Willa, and she'd always loved me, it was natural for us to be here, loving this man and each other. This, was meant to be.

The genie was uncorked.

I gathered my legs beneath me, hand still rubbing my spot and kissed him, then leaned up, presenting my breasts again. He nuzzled one and sucked it, until my nipple was hard—and I was tugging at my other nipple for him. Willa reached a hand up over to follow mine through my underwear, and started pushing up, right where I wanted her—him—either of them to be, the cotton keeping her out even as its wetness betrayed me.

We were all moving, all in motion, the bed rocking, their hips matching, my breasts bobbing as my hands rubbed more quickly. Then something happened—between them—I could feel the mood deepen. Gray pulled his mouth off my breasts and looked back down at Willa and her hands left me and went for his back. He started stroking in earnest, like everything that'd come before'd been mere practice, I could see all the flawless muscles in his ass and back clench as he went deeper with each stroke.

I lay down beside Willa then, pretending that each thrust he pushed into her was going into me, and I could see by the light of his desk lamp the way his stomach curved down and her stomach curved up for them to meet, where his shaft ran in and out of her, as her light fur hid the precise spot where they joined, where I most wanted to see. I rubbed myself in time with his strokes, with the sound of her voice rising, with his breathing heavy overhead, his streaming hair brushing both of us as he bucked himself deeper in.

Then her hand found mine and grasped it again, and I held it tight as I rubbed myself hard. She was going—and I wanted to go with her—with both of them—*oh god please yes, yes, yes!*

Willa came first, and it was like she was coming for the both of us —watching her spasm underneath him, her body curl as she gasped and cried out, watching her getting fucked—it dragged me along. I shouted out, the first time I'd ever been allowed to scream during orgasm, instead of muffling them in pillows at home—and I screamed again as another tremor rippled through me.

And over Willa, over both of us, was Gray, still fucking her like some sort of fuck-machine, watching the two of us, eyes intent and dark.

"Good," he said, and then growled. It was an animal sound, and he started thrusting more wildly, while she made helpless taken sounds. He growled again and grunted, thrusting fiercely up. I knew he was coming inside of her, and it made me *ache* to feel him—I wanted that so bad—the space between my legs had never felt half so hollow before. He grunted again, thrashing as she moaned, and then hissed, pulling himself out of her, the condom wrapped around him shining with her juices. He chuckled darkly and then moved to stand, walking across the room.

Willa moaned again and collapsed, and I lolled at her side, feeling almost as wrung out. It was like I'd gotten to go along on her ride—just like I always had—it made all this make sense.

She nuzzled her head against my shoulder and I moved my arm to hold her.

"That was so good," I whispered. "Better than it's ever been before."

She reached up to push a piece of hair out of my face. "I'm so glad you came."

"Me too," I said, kissing her gently.

I knew enough about how penises worked to know that we'd have to wait until Gray could go a second time. Even if he couldn't go —I had enough masturbation fantasies now for the rest of my life.

But really—I knew something had changed in me now. The genie was in the open. Even if Gray couldn't fuck me—I knew from here on out I was going to find some way to *be* fucked when I wanted it. Now that I knew who I was, now that I felt my own power—I wouldn't be denied again. Not even if we had to go out and buy Willa a strap-on. Actually—maybe that was a....

Gray returned from the vicinity of his desk and sat back down, legs splayed. His cock draped atop the large balls between his legs, thick and long.

"Come here, Angela."

I looked to Willa, who nudged me away, and then moved to do as I was told, crawling over to him, my small breasts dangling down.

"Give me your hand," he commanded.

I rocked back to kneel and put my hand out. He took it and sunk it down and with curious fingertips I stroked. The skin of his shaft was soft, but underneath it felt firm—was firming—his cock rose beneath my hand like some separate animal as I touched it, and I gasped in surprise. "But I thought," I whispered.

"You thought wrong," he answered, and took my hand, wrapping it around himself, and then drew it slowly up and down. I could feel the lip where the head of his cock began, the smooth underbelly of his shaft, and where it seamed with lower parts of him. And I knew without knowing what it would feel like to hold it inside of me, where all of my darkness ached.

Should I do what Willa'd done? I looked to him for answers and saw him regarding me coolly, waiting for me to make the next move. So I lowered my head slowly, bobbing down, using my other hand for balance as I opened up my mouth, licking him like he was an ice cream cone, sweeping my tongue over his head. He chuckled at that and rocked back on one arm, then let go of himself and started using that hand to size me up, grabbing at my breasts, reaching beneath to pull and rub my nipples with his fingers, then grabbing my rising ass, palming each cheek.

Memories triggered and I remembered a ranch my mom had sent me to one summer, where I'd watched a cowboy getting ready to break a mare—him testing her, feeling her all over, seeing if she was ready to be ridden. It felt similar to what was happening now, and at the thought of that, I brought both my lips around the head of him, to suck with intent, and spread my legs a little wider.

I was ready. God, I was so *fucking ready.*

And then Willa was there. Brave Willa, smart Willa. She wriggled around on her half of the bed until she was directly south of me and pushed her head between my knees. I paused on Gray's cock, still sucking his head like he was a monstrous lollipop, as she reached up to pull my hips down onto her face. I felt one of her hands moving my underwear out of the way and then—I felt her tongue lick up.

My labia parted for her, already dripping wet, and she knew where to kiss me, the spot where they met, where I'd just finished rubbing. I moaned—if her kissing me there made kissing Gray feel like that—I started sucking on him even harder, working on his penis with my tongue.

He groaned overhead and I groaned into him, trapped between arching back to let Willa have more of me, and rocking forward to take more of him. I liked the way he smelled, the scent of sex in the air, his own sweet musk, and the way he tasted, the glaze of cum he'd just spilled for Willa on my tongue in my mouth. Willa—kept finding—the right spot and—I pulled my head off of his cock to make an animal whine.

"Not without me you don't, girl." Gray said, pulling me to him and away from her. He tugged my underwear off, then snapped open another condom to unfurl it over himself. Then he grabbed me again and lay down, pushing us both further up the bed, as he held me to his chest.

It felt natural to lay beside him, so I did, as his lips met mine and started to kiss. Willa crawled up behind us and mirrored me, her breasts at my back, and I felt her hands wind around to touch mine, as his hand stroked down to grab my top leg and pull it over him. He twisted, going flat, and spun me with him like an alligator, keeping me on top. I was all too aware of how close his cock was to me. It was like it was radiating heat and I could feel where it was with any part of my body.

I knew I was so wet, and I knew exactly what I wanted—he kissed me, not moving my body or his, just stroking me with his hands, kissing under my chin, my jaw, down my neck, anywhere he could reach, as I kissed him back, anywhere I could. Then I saw Willa reach behind me, to keep stroking him, and I leaned over to kiss her, because she hadn't been forgotten but—

I *needed* this. I'd been aching for this for so long—it felt like years, decades, eons. All of time stretched out behind me, the time when I wasn't this woman—and now we were so close to the moment when I was.

I braced both hands on his chest and rose up and he watched me with a dark smile, giving nothing away. "Are you ready to beg me girl?"

I nodded helplessly. What use was pride when I was desperate to get fucked?

"Then do it," he said, his gaze steady on mine.

I licked my lips. "Please."

One of his eyebrows rose. "Please what?"

"Please fuck me."

He let out a low moan and his hands found my hips, tilting me forward, pushing me down against him. Either Willa helped, or his cock knew exactly where to go, I felt it just barely push in, then back out, in and out, almost just brushing against me. I wriggled, wanting more, wanting to be taken the same way he'd taken Willa, long and hard.

"Patience," he said, holding me still, bringing himself further up with his hips. I could feel the exquisite span of his stomach curving below me, reach back and feel the muscles in his ass rise, but only the tip of his head went in.

"More," I pleaded. "Before I die—more."

"No one's dying today," he said, but his hands on my hips tensed and pushed me further back and I felt my pussy parting, opening to let him in. *At last, at last, at last.* I gasped at the sensation and he moaned.

Willa reached up to trace my lips with her fingers, and I bit and sucked on one of them—and she pushed it further inside my mouth. I wanted him like I was taking her, surely he knew that—and I felt him stretch me wider.

"You're tight, princess," Gray said. "I don't want to hurt you. Don't move."

"Don't stop," I whispered, around Willa's finger.

And he didn't. He stayed there, gently pulsing—and I—with this complete stranger fucking me—I trusted him. It almost hurt. It wanted to hurt. But I wanted this so bad that I wouldn't let it—and the pain of him pushing in was transformed as my body moved past it, letting me envelope him. I whined as he stretched me and it hurt-right-good, I could feel him pushing, pushing up, claiming me inch by inch. It was as if he'd always belonged there, taking up this new space inside me that had never been filled by a man before.

"God," he growled, and I looked down and saw him through my sex-glazed eyes, his jaw clenched. I felt his hands tight on my thighs, and the rise of his ass beneath me, hitching up into my hips, and I realized how much he was holding back—and just what his restraint was costing him. So I clawed my hands into the muscles of his chest, and shoved myself back, sealing us tight, finishing it. I cried out as I pinned myself on him, feeling myself spread open to my widest point, all of my pussy wrapped around his cock.

"You're so beautiful, Angie," Willa whispered, coming up to kiss me as I shuddered on top of him. "You can do it, okay? You're so strong." She stroked my hair out of my face and cupped a breast. "You can take it. I know you can."

I made a whining sound and nodded, because she was right, because I could.

"You're so fucking tight, girl," Gray growled below me. "If I let myself go, I might tear you in two."

I full-body shivered at the thought of that, at some man needing me to the point of abandon, no matter how murderous. My nipples went hard, and I felt the fat head of his cock rub deep inside me as I moved.

"Yeah," he muttered, putting his hands around my waist to encourage me, rocking me back and forth in slow motion. "Just like that, girl. Get used to it. Get used to me fucking you."

Willa started kissing at my breasts, and I wound my arms around her, as if using her for strength, while Gray started taking bigger strokes.

It still burned, a little, but it also felt good, so good, better than I'd ever felt before—no late night furtively touching myself in my bedroom could compare, especially with Willa sucking at my nipples, and listening to Gray groan, as his thrusts started becoming stronger.

"I'm going to fuck your pussy hard soon, girl," he promised, "but I need you to come for me, first." He licked a thumb, set it between my thighs, and started in on my clit.

"Oh God," I whispered, as Willa laughed, switching breasts.

"God has nothing to do with it," Gray rumbled looking up, pulling himself nearly out of me, and then taking me in one stroke. I cried out. "Hurry, girl," he said, speeding his thumb up, using my wetness to rub me. "I want to fuck the shit out of you," he said, with a growl, speeding up.

I thrilled at the thought, even if I couldn't imagine anything better than this, right here and now.

"But I need to know you're ready," he went on, his jaw dropped. "I want to feel you grab me with your virgin cunt."

Under any other circumstance the foul word would've made my ears ring but here it felt right. Cunt, pussy, whatever he wanted to call it, as long as he kept shoving his cock inside of it—*just like he was* —it was his.

A weight sank between my hips as my stomach crunched and my ass tightened. I was going to—I was going to—I was going to—

"Yeah," he growled, and reached over to spank Willa's ass. She yelped and lightly bit my nipple and it was like that was the trigger.

I wrapped an arm around her head, keeping it there, making her suck on me as I shuddered, screaming, the tornado that I kept deep inside, finally set free. I writhed on Gray, speared by his cock, rubbing myself into his thumb, while at the same time I made the head of his cock hit the right spot inside and I cried out, wordlessly, again, and again, coming so hard I saw stars.

"*Oh my God!*" I shouted at the end, as the final wave pulled through me, and then I fell towards Willa, as if I'd been shot. Gray's cock yanked out of me, and through a haze of endorphins I vaguely realized he was still hard.

He laughed darkly, beside the two of us, stroking a rough hand down my back. "Good girl, Angela," he said encouragingly, then he leaned up on an elbow to pierce me with a stare. "But you're not done yet."

I panted over Willa, who had wrapped me in her arms. "No?" I asked, trying to catch my breath.

He shook his head and gave me a killer smile, before rising up onto his knees. Then he picked me up by the hips like I weighed nothing, and pulled me to all fours in front of him, over Willa. "Now that you're not a virgin anymore," he said, rubbing his palm up and down my ass, "let's see what you can do."

He shoved himself in me without preamble, all the way up to the fucking hilt, and I cried out at being filled so soon again. I could feel the natural curve of his cock pulling up inside of me, and as he started thrusting, I could feel the thickness of his head rub up and down my orgasm-swollen inner walls.

I moaned without thinking. I'd had no idea I could feel as good as I had before, and yet here I was—and I might get to feel that good again.

"Yeah," he said, in agreement with my moan. "You're still so fucking tight, Angela. And I love knowing I'm the first man to get to do this to you." He punctuated every other word with a thrust, and then made an animalistic sound—much like he had when he'd come for Willa. I stiffened and thrilled.

He was going to come for me—*if not now, soon!*—and I'd get to feel him shoving his cum deep inside me, claiming me, for all time.

And then Willa's hands were in my hair, pulling my mouth to hers. I thought for a moment that she might be jealous, but no—I could tell by her eyes she was thrilled for me. That she was with me —that we *both* got to be here.

"I want to see him fuck you every which way," she whispered. I gasped—and I could've sworn I could feel him getting harder inside. She licked her fingers and then reached between my legs to rub my clit.

"Oh God, Willa," I whispered back, biting my lips. My best friend was making an already hot moment impossibly hotter. How did she always know what to do? We'd read the same dirty books!

But she was always braver than me—until now.

"Do you know how hot it is to watch him ride you?" she asked sincerely, and I heard Gray groan. "To know what he's doing to you?"

I shook my head like a horse fighting reins, the weight of his cock thudding solidly in and out of me, her fingertips moving fast.

"I can't stand it anymore, it's so fucking hot," she breathed, and collapsed back, the hand that had been touching me now trapped between her own legs, as she pinched her nipple with the other hand.

Her legs were spread open, right in front of me, I could see every inch of her sex, the way her folds were just like mine, glistening with juices, like a ripe piece of fruit.

"Come here," I told her. Her eyes met mine, and for a second, disbelieved—and then she saw that I was serious and moved her hips over, so that I could bow my head down and feast.

Gray made an unholy sound behind me at seeing me go down on her. He grabbed my hips and shoved himself in deep, watching as I licked her open and kissed her clit. I had no idea what I was doing, so I tried to do what *I* liked, nibbling and pulling at her clit with my lips, tasting her with my tongue, until her hands were wound in my hair and I heard her whisper the words, "Suck it," with a whine, and a slowly added, "please."

I did as I was told and felt her relax back and open up, and then Gray started thrusting again, hard, which made each of his thrusts roll through me and into her.

She was salty and sweet, like all good candies rolled into one, and I reached my fingers in to spread her open so I could lick her madly, and sometimes push my tongue in, between sucks.

She rocked back, moaning, and I was moaning into her, and Gray started making his animal sounds. He put a hand on each of my ass cheeks, spreading every inch of me tight and wide, and I knew he was watching his cock slide in and out.

Everything felt so good and true. I was finally getting fucked like I'd always needed and somehow, miraculously, I'd managed to do it with—and get it done partially by—my best friend, which was fucking good, because if she weren't here now, I'd have never been able to explain all this to her.

"Angela," Willa said, her hands tightening in my hair, keeping my mouth on her clit. Feeling her tense, knowing she was close, heightened all of my sensations. I could feel the peaks of my nipples brushing the bed with each of Gray's thrusts, as I heard the solid smacking wetness where we met and felt the slap of his huge balls. "Ang—Ang—you're going to make me!" she promised, and then she *did*, yelping and shuddering, I could feel her orgasm rippling through her.

I followed her with my mouth, now gently kissing her down there the same as she'd earlier kissed my lips, until she rolled away, panting. Willa moved sideways, collapsed in front of me, reaching for one of my breasts. "Angela," she said softly, giving my name whole new shades of meaning.

Gray had slowed down to watch her come, but now that that was over, he was back in charge. He reached forward and caught his hand in my hair, pulling my head and body back while he thrust forward, pinning me back. "All sorts of firsts for you today, girl, hmm?"

"Uh huh," I agreed, my voice high, as I struggled to nod, reined by my hair.

"And now," he said, letting go of my hair, reaching down to grab me bodily and hoist me up against him. "You're all mine," he said low.

One of his hands was between my breasts and at my throat, the other pressed my hips back. His hips pulsed in short sharp pumps, and I found my knees spreading wider, to try to take more of him in.

"Good," he agreed with himself.

He curled over me then, holding himself up with one arm, while the other grabbed a breast—he was so much taller than me that he covered me completely. He was curved over my back and I could sense things taking a deliciously desperate turn as he started driving his cock deep. It was like after so long being careful he couldn't stand it anymore, he had to have me—*me!*—and part of me still couldn't believe it was happening, even as I felt his cock thrust in and then rip back out again.

I was sure I'd never been more wet, and at the thought of my pussy bringing this dangerous man low, I started making animal sounds to match his, my cries bouncing like my breasts did, in time with his thrusts.

"Fuck, girl, you make me *hard*," he growled. I saw his hand by my hand clenching into the sheets. "I want to explode inside you, but I also never want fucking you to end." He said it almost like it was a complaint, that anyone should ever have so much control over him.

I threw my head back, as much as I could, and arched my ass up so my pussy could keep taking more of him. I'd never felt more like an animal than at that moment, like I was getting mounted by something wild.

Everything felt electric—each stroke of his hard cock, opening me wide and shoving in again—my breasts bouncing, his balls slapping—Willa watching in wide-eyed amazement at me getting fucked. She raced a hand back to touch me, but I didn't need it—I would've come without it—just from him fucking me. I knew, as a woman knows, that he needed to own me, that he was dying to fill me up, and I knew I wanted to be filled. It felt like that until this moment my entire life I'd been an empty cup.

Heat welled. My stomach muscles bunched, my ass tightened, and my nipples almost burned where Willa touched them. The orgasm I'd had before—it would be nothing compared to this one, it was bearing down on me like a freight train, driven by his cock.

I opened my mouth to say a warning and then screamed instead. That was all there was time for—and then it was on me—like I'd been jumped. My orgasm made everything tense and pull, making me grab the sheets and grab him as I shouted incoherently. I curled up with the force of it, and his hips followed mine, as his mouth bit my shoulder—almost to hang on. He made a savage sound and I knew he was losing himself inside me as my pussy throbbed, pulsing tight. His hips bucked of their own accord then, a wild staccato, and his animal need would've driven his seed deep if there hadn't been a condom in the way.

And deep was where I wanted to take it. I already knew Gray was right—no other man could ever fuck me like this again—and as our hips danced, the ends of our orgasms fraying at the edges, I couldn't begin to imagine giving this up.

He grunted a final time, gave a final thrust, and then slid out of me with a gasp. I felt bereft at once, and all that was in me wanted to start planning how to get him back in.

But my body was too tired, no matter my mind. I fell forward onto the bed into Willa's waiting arms and he fell beside us both, breathing hard. It felt like an eternity passed before he rolled over and looked down.

"You're both perfect," he said, dark eyes deadly serious. Willa laughed.

I blinked, dazed, and I hadn't caught my breath yet—but I knew two things for sure, laying there between them, as he'd fucked every other thought from my mind—that I was incontrovertibly in love with both of them and that I would *not* be going back home tonight.

CHAPTER NINE
ANGELA

I woke up the next morning to an empty bed and the sound of muffled groaning. Gray had showed us last night where the bathroom was, cleverly hidden behind the bed, palatial, as if a woman had planned it out. After a walk around the room wearing a sheet like a robe, I deduced that that was where the groaning was coming from. Setting my ear against the wood paneling the sounds got louder, clearly Willa, and I heard soft grunts, clearly Gray.

She was enjoying herself. Again. I had no idea how she was managing it, I was almost chafed, and my hips were beyond sore from everything I'd gotten them into last night.

The temptation to walk in on them though and join them again —after everything we'd done—I shook my head to break the spell and walked around the room.

There was a closet on the wall nearest the bathroom. I opened it slowly and found a rack of shirts and leather. Everything smelled like Gray and I wanted to fall in. I thumbed through the clothes instead, surprised to find two dresses hanging at the closet's far end, one in floral blue, the other with a pattern that looked like rain drops. I closed the door quietly and went to inspect Gray's desk.

It had a line of pulpy paperbacks stacked at the back—the male equivalent of the trashy romance novels Willa and I gleefully read. I pulled one out to read about the cop who was undoubtedly going to solve a murder against all odds and found it inscribed.

For my baby. Love, Brittani.

Clearly, there had been a recent ex-girlfriend, after all—the one we'd been busy fucking from his thoughts all night. And from the sound of things in the bathroom, Willa was doing an extra special job erasing her now. I went to Gray's jeans, fished out his wallet, and found out his real name was Erik—then Willa's voice started to rise. I tucked the wallet back into his jeans and stood up, walking toward the bathroom door.

I could hear her, almost feel her, urging him on. Her voice was louder, the sounds now more wild, echoing against the tile—I imagined them in the shower, him rutting behind her, her barely holding on against the wall. The way she was screaming, he was either killing her or fucking her, I didn't know which—I only knew if it was the latter she'd kill *me* if I interrupted them.

Willa's final scream rang out and then I heard Gray give a long, low groan as he finished himself inside her. Listening to them—the urgency of my own unmet need made me sway. Then the door swung open unexpectedly and I was caught eavesdropping as he walked out. He closed the door and looked surprised.

"She's alive, right?" I said, kidding-not-kidding.

His eyebrows rose and then he laughed. "Yeah. Of course. We just didn't want to wake you," he said, giving me a guilty grin.

I shrugged like I didn't mind. And I wasn't jealous, really—just hungry still. I wondered if I'd always be hungry, from here on out. He walked by me and grabbed his jeans to pull on.

"Are you going somewhere?"

"Don't worry, I'll be back," he said, buckling his belt, then going into his closet for a shirt. Him leaving was a reminder that the outside world existed. One night out with Willa I could lie away, but one night and a morning, I wouldn't manage. I started looking for my own clothes, too. "Wait—what're you doing?" he asked.

"You're not the only one who has places to be—" My parents must have been mad with worry, I needed to go and talk them down.

He crossed the room back to me and caught my hands. "Don't— don't go. I've just got some club business to attend to. After that though, I'll bring food back for us. You can help yourself to anything behind the bar in the meantime. Just wait for me, okay?"

Looking up at him, it was impossible not to remember everything that'd happened the prior night. "Okay," I breathed.

"Good. I'll be right back," he said, and grabbed his vest.

The second he left I locked the door behind him, which was where Willa caught me when she came out. "Oh my gosh, Angie," she said, falling into the bed naked. I scurried back to her, almost tripping on the sheet.

"Willa—what the hell are we doing here?" I asked, mounting the bed to sit beside her.

She looked up at me with her post-orgasmic glow and caught my waist with a lazy arm. "Living the dream," she said, snuggled up against me, and fell back asleep.

WILLA WAS braver sleeping than I was awake. I kept trying to figure out ways to make my old world and this world mesh—they were like puzzle pieces that would never fit. But since I was already in trouble I might as well stay and keep ignoring the likely frantic messages my mother was leaving me.

I freed myself from Willa's arm, took an unfortunately solo shower, and then found all the clothes I'd worn yesterday, pulling them back on. I was thirsty—and some biker had promised me free beer.

I crept out into the hallway and heard an intermittent hum, like a refrigerator going bad. There couldn't be that many people at the bar right now, I mean it was early afternoon and—I turned the corner and saw a shirtless man leaning over a table on his elbows, and another man sitting behind him, the bartender from last night. He glanced up as I walked in and the humming stopped.

"So you survived."

"Seems so." I padded towards the back of the bar, where I was sure I'd find something in a bottle or can, making sure I was still close enough to the room to run back inside and throw the latch.

He snorted, and went back to the man in front of him. The humming began again, and the shirtless man winced.

I ducked below the bar and opened up a mini-fridge to grab a PBR. Then I popped back up like a nervous gopher. I shouldn't have worried though, all of the bartender's concentration was on the man's back, and the shirtless man was squinting in pain too tightly to see me.

I opened the can and heard its crisp sigh over the hum. I took a defiant glug, daring the bartender to stop underaged-me, and when he didn't I started sidling in his direction, craning my neck to see what was going on.

He was giving the shirtless man a tattoo. There was an array of inks behind him, primary colors and three different shades of gray and black.

"Don't worry, you'll get your chance," he said, without looking up.

I took a step closer. I wanted to see. The man was getting the outline of a massive snarling wolf in the center of his upper back.

"My chance as him, or as you?"

The bartender pulled back and looked at me dolefully. "You think you can draw?"

"I know I can."

"Then draw something for me."

I looked around the bar for inspiration. "What?"

"I don't know—something good." He reached behind himself and shoved a piece of paper my way. I took it, and ran back into the room for Gray's desk.

Gray's desk had three drawers—the first one was full of pens, pencils, and scraps of paper, the second two were locked. I sketched out my own version of the barman's snarling wolf, shading it in with the sides of pencils, while listening to Willa's snores. When I returned to him, he was almost done, taping a bandage over the man's back.

He took the art from me for inspection as the man left the bar. "Decent."

"Good," I corrected him.

"You scared of needles?"

"No."

He nodded slowly and appraised me again. "You can draw on paper, but can you draw on a man?"

"Uh...." I'd drawn on myself before. Show me an artist who hadn't. But....

Sensing my discomfort, he laughed. "Yeah, that's what I thought. Want to try?"

Before I could answer, he was rolling back one sleeve and showing me a hairy arm, with a scar scored down the middle, and grabbing for a razor. I watched in slight horror as he shaved a patch clean—and then in fascination as he changed out his tattoo gun's needles.

I wanted to say, *What, no, you're kidding, right?* But I also wanted to call his bluff—there was no way someone like him was going to let someone like me ink them, first time out. So instead of protesting, I decided to see how far he'd let things go.

"What's your name?"

"Angela. Yours?"

"Wade. And you can have a square inch," he said, looking over at me, his smug expression a clear dare.

"What do you want?"

"Dealer's choice."

I thought of the tritest tattoo I could. "Fine, then you're getting a heart with a Mom."

He chuckled. "Feel free," he said, and handed me the tattoo gun.

I looked at the inks he had lined up—he hadn't cleared away the old inks yet, but reusing those seemed unsanitary. I'd set up palettes before—I could do this. I put the gun down and arranged red and black in little plastic wells, then faced him.

He wasn't that much older than Gray, but something in his bearing said he'd seen a rougher life. His dark hair was slicked back in a severe fashion, making a crisp widow's peak on his forehead. He scooted down the table and lay his arm out. I took his spot and tapped my foot on the foot pedal, listening to the gun, feeling it buzz like I was holding a hummingbird.

"Get the ink on it—there—go," he prompted, shoving his arm near.

This had to be some joke, but I couldn't stop now—the thought of putting art on someone else—*in someone else*, in a manner of speaking—the allure was too grand.

"Come in at an angle. Don't stab," he said, and I stopped wondering when he would stop me and leaned forward.

With one fine needle I made a delicate outline, a symmetrical freehand heart, harder to do than it sounds. The bartender sat like a rock, a stark contrast to the man who'd been wincing before, and he was as intent on my art as I was. There was no way not to be close to him like this, him in my personal space, or he in mine, close enough to touch me, just as I was touching him, holding his skin taut with my free thumb.

When I was done with the outline, I pulled back and he raised his arm to look at it closely. "Not half bad."

"Thanks," I said, relinquishing the gun. Then I realized I'd forgotten to leave space for the scroll where 'Mom' would go, and started cursing, and he laughed.

"Don't worry about that. I'm not gonna let you fill it in. I'm too manly for a red heart, but the hair'll cover the outline soon. And there's no way I'd let you try lettering on me, not without practicing a ton first."

I heard the sound of a bike coming near and then parking as the engine shut off, and Gray walked in, holding a bag. At seeing Wade and I close, his eyebrows rose.

"Been teaching your girl a trade," Wade said.

Gray smiled at the both of us, half-wicked, half-sweet. "I hope it made her hungry."

"It did," I said, standing quickly, crossing the room to him. Gray took my hand and gave Wade a look, before pulling me back to his bedroom. I didn't realize until hours later I'd forgotten my PBR.

MY PARENTS WERE, as you might imagine, pissed. They'd just come to grips with the thought of me leaving for college, so finding out where I was really spending my time—and where Willa and I quickly started living—if I hadn't been eighteen, they would've come and 'rescued' me, by taking me home and chaining me to my bed.

But Willa and I knew we'd found true love, the kind you only read about, that blotted every other thought from your mind, just like a good high.

I kept going to school, taking the bus in, or on more thrilling days riding the back of Gray's bike, while Willa made a rough attempt at it, dropping all but her easiest classes, working at the Cash 4 Gold store at the end of the strip mall. Going back and forth to UNLV felt like a tunnel between two realities, the world that everyone else participated in, and the world at the bar with Gray and Willa that was mine. None of the boys on campus could even begin to tempt me from either of their sides, they all seemed like children comparatively. Whereas being with Willa and Gray every night—the knowledge of each other only we could share—seemed to make me wise.

The real world only interrupted infrequently, one: during one of my mother's anxious weekly phone calls, and two: when once a month most, but not all, of the Pack left for the Farm for a night, to take care of Pack business. And anything that was Pack business, Willa and I were not to know. We'd begged Gray to let us in—we'd held nothing back, so him having secrets felt unfair.

"You know how to have fun without me. So just stay in here and lock the door."

The first month that made sense, and the second, and the third, but by the fourth—"Please, Gray," Willa pleaded, but he was adamant.

"What do you think they're doing out there?" she asked me, after he was gone.

I had guesses but I wanted them to be wrong. Gray didn't have a 'real' job—I knew enough to know I didn't really want to know how he made money. "I don't know."

"I'm going to the bar," she said, unlocking the door and stomping out.

I followed her. Wade was behind the bar, with only a smattering of the local set left behind. Willa went over to pick all the songs she liked on the jukebox.

"How's school?" he asked. The hair on his arm had indeed covered up my thin heart.

"It's all right." I shrugged.

He leaned over the bar toward me. "You still curious about my guns?"

"Focus on the task at hand, Wade," Daziel, another older pack member, reminded him.

"Yeah, yeah," Wade said, blowing him off, setting up a row of shot glasses, filling them to the brim with tequila. After a moment's hesitation, he pulled out two more to top off.

"Them too?" Daziel asked.

"Why not? They're suffering as much as the rest of us." He pulled something else out from behind the bar after that, a bottle with an eyedropper. I tensed, but he put it into every shot glass, the clear fluid he squirted instantly blending in.

At some appointed time Willa and I were not a party to, all the men came up. She and I hovered at the far side of the bar, and Wade shoved over our shots. "To the Pack!" he shouted, and as one, the men drank. Willa and I did too, or tried too—I sputtered in pain.

"Fuck, Wade," Willa said, coming up with a smile, even though her shoulders hunched like she was wounded. "That needs lime and salt."

"Lime and salt's for pussies," he said, leaning over to top her shot off.

THE THIRD TIME that threw me out of our little perfect life was when Gray came home late one night, covered in blood.

Willa was out at the club with the other girls, under Nikki's watchful supervision. She was like the Pack's den mother, not much older than we were, but you could feel that she *belonged* in a way that Willa and I didn't yet. She was able to get anyone in to any club, anywhere in Vegas, even when you were under twenty-one, a talent that Willa made frequent use of, while I was home studying, books and laptop open on Gray's desk.

Gray stayed out late fairly often, but usually we could tell when something like this was coming up, there was a tension in the air, an urgent need to act. Sometimes, beforehand, he acted out on us, fucking us so wildly we almost couldn't come up for air, other times we acted on each other, holding each other close and quietly, neither one of us wanting to say aloud what we were thinking: '*What the hell had we gotten ourselves into again?*' But then the storm would break and it was easy to convince yourself that that storm was the last.

I was unprepared for him to come home looking like that that night though, his arrival startled me.

"Oh my God—Gray—are you okay?" He strode across the room and started shedding clothing while I hovered nearby. "What happened?" I pressed.

"You don't want to know."

"I do."

"Then I don't want you to know," he said, going into the bathroom. I heard the shower turn on as I leaned against the door.

I never knew what to do in times like these. To take him at his word? Or show him that we had something I thought was worth fighting for—even if fighting meant ignoring what he'd said? I hovered nervously and then started taking off my clothes—I knew the fastest way to make everything peaceful again. I opened the bathroom door, steam billowing out.

Gray stood in the open shower, hidden by only a half-wall of glass and tile. Red streaks were staining down his back.

"You're hurt," I breathed.

He looked over at me angrily. "I'll be fine."

For all that he thought he knew what was best for everyone, all the time, why could he never see when he needed caring? I picked up a washcloth and walked near. "Just...." I began.

He made a growling sound but didn't move as I came up behind him and started patting it at his back. The edges of a single bullet wound were puckering, like it was old, even though the blood said it was fresh. It'd heal and scar soon and be just another thing about Gray that I would never understand.

"You're still innocent. I want to keep you that way," he said, turning toward me, pushing the washcloth away.

"Why?" I asked, looking up at him as the shower rained down on us both.

"So every time I fuck you is like the first time," he said, pushing me back against the wall.

I ran my hands into his hair as his body pressed against mine, our mouths locked on one another's. His hands searched up and down my sides, pulling my hips towards his, making me feel his hard-on between my thighs.

We were too good at this by now to take long—I spread my legs and arched forward as he pushed up, his cock finding home—and— no condom. I was on birth control, but still, no condom—his cock slid in as he groaned, and I knew I didn't care. I wanted to be his, skin to skin.

"This is how I wanted it," he panted, feeling it as I did, a strange new closeness between us. All I could do was nod as he pulled one of my legs up, to reach himself deeper inside me. His other hand caught my wrist and planted it over my head, against tile. "How I've always wanted it," he murmured.

I tried to move my trapped hand and found I couldn't—but I could use the anchor he'd given me by pinning it to curl myself up on my toes and—my free hand wound around his neck for balance, as he pulled my bent leg closer still.

In his kinder moments, Gray would ask things like, *'How is that?'* and *'Is this going to work for you?'* But I knew I'd caught him off-guard here and made an offering of myself, and that's how he was going to take me. He leaned into the wall, into me, pounding into my pussy with swift smooth strokes. My free hand clawed up his back like whatever had just hurt him, my mouth kissing and biting his chest, his shoulder, and his lips were on my neck and everything spun together, the water raining down on us both, making me feel like I was drowning in him all over. Still thrusting, he leaned down and touched his forehead to mine.

"I'm gonna cum inside you, Angela."

I nodded so he could feel it as I whispered, "Okay." His grip on my wrist and thigh tightened and I felt off balance as he pulled me into him, while pushing both of us back against the wall—I heard him suck in a breath, his whole body tensing, ready to shove me full of his cum—and at the thought of him finally unloading himself into me at long last—I teetered on my standing leg and reached down and rubbed and—just as his hips jerked and his cock bobbed I came with a howl, throbbing against him bodily.

"Yeah, Angie-girl," he said, pinning me up on his jetting cock as I spasmed and took it from him. "Yes—that—that," he growled, into my ear.

He freed me slowly, leg first, then wrist, kissing me madly, lips, neck, and chest, making my nipples stand at attention, as I felt his load drip out of me, the water carrying it away.

Then with a burst of cold air the door was open and Willa standing there, looking between us with a mischievous grin. "What did I miss?"

Gray looked at her over his shoulder. "Nothing you're not going to get from me next."

The night went on, and I never did find out who'd shot him.

CHAPTER TEN
ANGELA

Not long after that, I found Willa's birth control pills in the trash. I pulled them out and confronted her. "What the hell are you thinking?"

She pushed my accusatory hand aside. "I'm thinking that I want to get knocked-up."

She was so matter-of-fact about it, I was stunned. "Did you tell him?"

"Yeah."

"And he...agreed?"

She laughed at me, gently. "Yeah. Angela—if you were here more, you'd know. Look around. All the other girls—they're all somebody's mom or sister. Like everyone here is really inbred, in a good way, you know? Jamie's got Jonah, and they have little Danny, and Nikki's Daziel's girl, and they've got their twins—everyone here is tight, like family."

I already had a family—and was scheduled for another call from my mother on Tuesday night. But Willa didn't, and I knew how often she'd had to hide from her drunken father. "I like this," she went on. "I want to be a part of it. All the way."

"But how'll you support it?"

"Duh—Gray will help me. And you." She smiled innocently up at me. "Won't you?"

I sagged to sit beside her on the bed. "Yeah—of course."

"Thanks," Willa said, beaming. "I mean, you could have one too, and then they could both be the same age and—"

"Maybe," I said, to cut her off, while giving her a tight smile.

AFTER THAT, Willa and Gray needed some alone time.

I mean, it wasn't like we'd never been alone before that—sometimes one of us wouldn't be up for playing, or someone might've gone out—but this was the first time I felt explicitly excluded, made worse by the fact that they were going to the Farm.

It was Gray's suggestion—and Willa felt bad. "It's just for a night," she said. "I'm not even packing anything."

"I know," I said, trying to seem brave. "I get it."

"We'll be back soon," Gray said before kissing me, seemingly oblivious to my plight.

They took the Pack's communal car that sat outside, keys in the ignition, doors always unlocked, because it wasn't like anyone would dare steal it, and I waved as they drove off.

I trudged back into the bar hang-dog, heading for my schoolwork in the back, when Wade blocked my way. "Just because they're not here doesn't mean you need to be alone."

"No, but I'm really not in the mood, Wade."

"Are you sure? I got you a present." He offered out a box with a bow.

I took it from him, looking up. His eyes were crinkled, considering me. "Thanks."

"Open it."

I tugged the bow off and opened it up. Inside, two tattoo guns were nestled against foam. They were beautiful, their metal oxidized blue. "Wade," I breathed.

"I got tired of you borrowing mine."

"Thank you!" I closed the box and jumped him for a hug. He startled and then held me back, just a second too long, like he was out of practice.

"You're welcome. But you know what that means now—"

"What?"

He turned toward the rest of the bar. "Fresh meat!"

I'd been watching Wade tattoo for months, and he'd been supervising me for weeks, showing me the best ways to translate my artistic skills to skin. I'd done a number of small designs on assorted Pack members and their friends—there was always someone looking for a cheap tattoo—but I needed someone new to try these guns on.

"Murphy...." Wade cajoled, as a stout man came in from the back patio.

Sensing something was up, he said, "What? No."

"You wanted me to touch up your girlfriend just last week. Let Angela have a roll."

I knew Murphy had a wide image of a woman across his back. I hadn't known it was personal.

"She's the boss's bitch," Wade said.

Murphy snorted, unimpressed. "I ain't letting her mark me until she's got our marks."

Wade turned to me. "He does have a point."

I swallowed. My skin was just mine, so far. But every member of the Pack had a tattoo somewhere that'd give them away. I'd already seen a few bruised and bloody members earn theirs from Wade.

I looked around the bar. The rough world here—it was my world too. And if Willa was going to go and get herself knocked up, then I had to stay. I didn't go out and party with the others like she did, so it was natural for them to wonder about my loyalty.

Did I want them? Did they want me?

I wanted Gray. And Willa.

"Where?" I asked.

Wade grinned broadly. "Usually we blood in blood out. But seeing as you're Gray's...." Wade said, talking to himself.

"Somewhere she can see," Daziel said, coming over with a drink in hand.

"Somewhere *we* can see," Murphy grunted.

"All right," Wade agreed. And then he reached for my tank top and stretched it down and out. "Right here," he said, placing a hand on one breast where it curved up. "And here," he said, touching the other one."

"That'll do," Murphy agreed, and within minutes, Wade's kit was set up.

I SAT AS STILL as I could. I won't lie—it hurt. Each time the needles lifted it felt like I could breathe, and when they fell again I gritted my teeth.

I didn't even know what Wade was tattooing, and he was free-handing besides—but soon it became apparent that I was getting a wolf print on each breast—like a wolf had stood up and was pushing me down. When he switched out the needles to start filling in his outlines, Murphy brought me a drink—and then drank it in front of me.

"Don't be an ass, Murph," Wade said. Murphy laughed and offered me the other half the bottle.

"Unlike you, I can be sober and get a tattoo," I said through clenched teeth. Wade pulled off the needles to laugh.

"Only because I'm going to have to be black out drunk before I let you touch me," Murphy grumbled.

It didn't go down quite like that—although whether Wade was 'keeping him still' or 'holding him down' was debatable—but I did get to use my new guns on him, and they were just as smooth as I'd hoped they'd be. And that night I fell into bed alone with a quiet satisfaction, with the sheets off so my blood couldn't stain them.

CHAPTER ELEVEN
ANGELA

The next morning, Willa and Gray returned. He was happy—with her—and with me. He wanted to see the tattoos himself and I could tell he was pleased. The second after he kissed us both and went into the shower, I pounced Willa for information.

"Tell me everything. Now."

"We went out to the middle of a forest. There's all this land, and trees—it's not desert anymore over there."

"You went camping?" Suddenly the Farm seemed less sexy.

"No—there's a huge house in the center. We went inside, and he showed me around, and then we started making out—"

"Yeah?"

"And then we got high."

I double-blinked. "What?"

"Sometimes high sex is fun, Angie."

"No, I know, keep going—"

She gave a tiny shrug and a quirky smile. "And then we smoked out and fucked. All night. Like—he was hard like you wouldn't believe. He couldn't keep it out of me—he'd come, and then he'd hold me and we'd talk and then we'd fuck and he'd come again—

he like never pulled out. And I lost track of how many times I came."

"Wow," I said.

"Yeah," she agreed.

"Do you feel, uh…." I started, waving at her body.

"Oh my gosh, it's only been like twelve hours, silly," she said with an eye roll. "I am tired though. Nap with me?"

I'd been up late too. "Sure," I said, spooning her loosely.

WILLA WAS PREGNANT. Whether it was that night or some other—within a week she was bent over the toilet each morning. The other girls fawned on her, Nikki and Jamie and everyone else, offering advice, and they all seemed to know better than I did. Willa was right, the few women of the Pack did all seem to be moms.

And Gray changed, too. When he fucked us, he did so cautiously. Like Willa—and I—might break. If I were born a gentler person—or if I'd been initiated into sex any other way—I might have liked that, but as it was, his kindness felt misplaced. Especially because when he wasn't in our bed, he was distant—the transition between the two, attentive lover and distracted father-to-be was jarring.

"He just doesn't know what to do," Willa said, making excuses for him again. Her arm was around me and I was nestled up against her shoulder. Her stomach had started to swell and I thought her breasts were getting larger. "He'll come around."

I laced my fingers through hers. "He'd better."

WILLA STARTED HAVING contractions on the day of the Farm trip five months later. I could feel them rippling across her stomach, as she grit her teeth with each forceful squeeze.

"Hang on," I told her, grabbing my purse, helping her for the door. The car was out back, there was a hospital nearby—why hadn't we gone in to get her care sooner? I knew we were poor, but we weren't dumbfucks—

Gray blocked the back door. "You can't," he said, with a head shake.

"Why not?" I asked, as Willa tensed beside me.

"Because she'll be fine." He leaned down and picked her up, carrying her back to our bedroom as I chased behind.

"This isn't like you rolling in with some gunshot, Gray! There's another life at stake!" I shouted, as he set her back in bed.

"I know that, all right? But you just have to trust me. She doesn't need a doctor."

"She does!"

Torn between the two of us, what could Willa do?

"I'm gonna be okay. They're small—they're getting better—I read online this happens sometimes—"

"See?" Gray said.

"No, I don't—" I said, but he was already walking out the bedroom door.

I followed him out into the bar, where the Pack was getting ready to depart.

"I have Pack business, Angela," Gray said, knowing I was on his heels.

"What *business* do you have that could *possibly* be more important than her safety?"

The room went quiet as Gray turned—and hit me. Open handed, I could feel the weight from cheek to jaw. Then he pointed over my shoulder to Wade. "Don't let them go," he said, then turned. The bar emptied out behind him while I stood there, stunned, one hand coming up to trace my pain.

I ran back to the bedroom and dove into bed with Willa as Wade called out my name.

"What's wrong?" she asked, holding her arms out to me. I instinctively crawled into them.

"Gray hit me," I said, still startled by the truth of it.

Willa knew all about being hit by men. "Oh my God, really?" Willa said, touching my hot cheek with her hand.

"Yeah," I said, lips quivering, about to cry. It felt like everything we'd had here for the past year was starting to crumble. "Are you okay?"

"Yeah. They've stopped. I'm better now. Are you okay?"

The shock of getting hit was fading, replaced by anger at the affront of it. "I don't know," I answered, truthfully.

"I'm so sorry, Angie. If I'd known how this was going to divide us, I never would've done it," she said, putting her hand atop her stomach.

I sobbed into her shoulder, but met her hand with my own. "It isn't the baby's fault. And even if it's half his, it's still half yours."

Her fingers laced with mine and squeezed. "The good half."

CHAPTER TWELVE
ANGELA

I heard the door open the next morning while Willa held me tight. Gray came into the room, standing at the foot of the bed. I glared up at him and he jerked his head toward the bar, before leaving. I crept out of bed to follow him, leaving Willa still sleeping.

"I came home early to see you—and check in on her. Is she okay?"

"Do you actually care?" I snarled at him.

His eyes pierced me. "More than you know," he growled low. The bar was empty, except for the two of us. He got himself a drink, and had the gall to offer me one. "I can't have you disrespect me in front of my men, Angie. Ever." His voice was quiet. Half the strip-mall was full of make-shift Pack member living quarters, like a Nevernever Land for the motorcycled insane.

"Then take me somewhere where I can disrespect you, because I have some *disrespecting* to do," I quietly hissed.

His eyebrows rose but he opened up the coat room to toss me a helmet. "Gear up."

On the back of his bike, clinging to him, it was easy to remember all the reasons I'd fallen for him. Being here felt wild, the wind ripping through my hair, the rumbling of a metal beast between my thighs—but Gray made it safe. Plausible, really, that it was me, here, doing this, on some crazy adventure I'd embarked on with my best friend a year ago. His shoulders blocked the worst of the wind and he was doing all the driving—all I had to do was hold on.

He took us away from Vegas entirely, out and up, for over an hour, until the sun was overhead and we were on a barely paved road winding up a mountain, between massive trees.

"Where are we?" I asked, after he pulled over and I hopped off.

"The Farm. Part of it." He took off his helmet, and half-leaned, half-sat on his bike. "Feel free to disrespect me now," he said, giving me a smirk.

I drew myself up in front of him, drawing my anger quickly to hand. "How *dare* you hit me. And how *dare* you play games with Willa—and the baby. Your baby!"

He nodded, his face a closed book, watching me. "Is that it?"

I looked around here, trapped, with no way home but him. "No. It's just—why would you let us get involved with you if you weren't going to take *us* seriously?"

His brow arched. "You think I don't take you seriously? Angie, you have no idea how seriously I take you—"

"Because you never tell me! Or Willa! What goes on up here, what happens on all those other *business* nights—"

"I'm trying to keep you—to keep our family—safe."

"From what?" I shouted at him. He closed his mouth around whatever he'd been about to say next and looked wounded. "Jesus, Gray, if you can't tell me the truth now—how long do you think I'm going to stick around to listen to lies?"

"I don't enjoy lying to you!" he shouted back. "I don't want to. But I have to. There are some things you're just not meant to know!"

I'd started crying somewhere, having scratched through the scab of my anger into a deep depressive well. "Why're you always holding back from me? What—what changed?"

"Angie," he groaned.

"We used to be so close." I walked over to him, trying to see the man I wanted there. "It seemed like everything was going to work out and—I don't know, did I grow up? Did you pull away? Or...both?"

"I never pulled away," he said, even as he took a step back.

"You did!" I protested. "After—once Willa got pregnant—you *did*. She's felt it too."

His eyes clouded, as if in pain—like someone was twisting a knife in his side. "If that's the case, I'm sorry. I didn't mean to. You both mean the world to me."

"It doesn't feel like that anymore, Gray. It feels like," I said and started shaking my head, disbelieving that I ever could've been so dumb as to believe us three would work. "Like you don't trust me. Or her."

"Baby," he said, staring down at me, mirroring my head shake with his own. "I don't trust anyone."

It stunned me to hear the truth at last—but it was true, wasn't it? Why he kept us at an arm's length, even when we were close enough to fuck. Willa and I—we might as well have been in love with a ghost.

"But I want to," he said, softly. He took a step over and put a hand out for me. I stared at him, measuring him with my eyes, then I took it, letting him pull me close, to hold me.

"Do you mean that?" I murmured into his chest.

"I do," he said, stroking my hair back as he held me possessively.

All around us silence reigned—we were in the middle of nowhere, the only sound a distant birdsong. I rested my head against his t-shirt, where I could hear the beating of his heart.

I wanted it to beat for me.

His hand came up and took hold of my chin, pulling my mouth towards his. I went with the movement, rising up on my toes, wanting to taste forgiveness on his lips and feel honesty from his tongue. My hands rose to encircle his shoulders, to pull his head further down to me, winding my fingers in his hair. His head pulled back, and his lips left mine, kissing my nearest wrist instead.

"Angie," he whispered.

"Yeah?" I whispered back, both of us close enough to share the same breath.

"I have to have you," he said, setting his forehead against mine. "Please. Now."

I couldn't remember another time when he'd asked. "Yeah," I breathed back, and felt his hands fall to my waist.

After that, it was a dance to see how quickly we could take our clothes off, while still touching one another. I was working on my shirt and bra when he picked me up, himself half-naked, carrying me into the woods beside the road, leaving the bike and our boots behind. He found a field of spring clover behind a tree and put me there, unbuckling his jeans while I squirmed out of my shirt and tossed it aside. Once his jeans were pushed down far enough, his cock came out, as eager to feel me as I was to feel it. His body bent over mine and I ran my hands up the muscles of his stomach and over his shoulders, lacing my fingers behind his neck.

"This is the way I want to be with you, every night," he said, staring into my eyes as I spread my legs for him, and I could already feel the tip of him pressing up and in. And as he bent his head down to kiss me, he pushed in and began to thrust.

I wrapped my legs around him, my heels against his back—now that he was in me, I wanted to keep him there. His hips pulsed against mine, pushing me back into the soft dirt, and I made little whines in response, as his cock found its home inside me. Other than that though, we were quiet, just the soft sounds of fucking and being fucked.

"You're so good to me, Angie. You and Willa both. I never would've imagined—that I could feel like this," he crooned with each new stroke. I closed my eyes and rolled my head back, feeling him inside and out, as he finally said all the words I wanted to hear. "I don't want you to ever leave me."

"I won't," I whispered, catching a fresh hand in his hair.

"Promise?"

"Yeah," I breathed.

"Good. Because I am going to keep you—right—here—" he said, then started pumping hard, and I cried out, in surprise, but also in recognition. This was the Gray that I'd fallen for, the one with over-whelming strength, who knew what he wanted to take. "I just—need to do this—I need you Angela—all of me needs you—and I've waited—so long," he growled, and then arched his hips in on a thrust. I felt his body shudder over me like it had a hundred times before, as he spilled his cum so deep—and then an entirely new sensation, as parts inside me were spread wide.

"Gray!" I shouted. He covered me with his body, his elbows on either side of my shoulders.

"Go with it, Ang," he whispered hoarsely in my ear, still stroking slowly, deep inside. I knew he'd come, but he was still hard, and I was so tight.

"What the—" I began, fighting panic.

"Shh, shh," he whispered, catching my head in his hands, staring into my eyes. "I love you, Angie."

"I—I—" I began, pinned on the ground, helpless, with a moun-tain rocking over me and between my legs. "I love you too," I confessed, because it was true.

And inside me, his cock—always at the ready, no matter how many times Willa and I drained it—seemed impossibly hard, and thicker besides. Was this what'd happened with Willa at the Farm, during their orgiastic night? I brought my feet back down to push off the ground and into him.

He groaned and started stroking faster, the majority of him always inside me. "Yeah—that's good."

It was. The way he rose over me, the new width of his cock, even if it was all in my head—all of my nerves felt shiny and tight, like a string ready to be plucked. Then he leaned down and licked my left breast. A jolt of power ran through my body to my hips.

"More," I demanded—and he caught my nipple in his mouth, looking up at me as I writhed beneath him. His tongue stroked my nipple and, "More, more, more," I begged. He chuckled into my soft flesh and bit me gently, leaving me gasping, as my hips started taking what they needed from his cock. His head rose, letting the stubble of his beard graze across me, and then he went for my other breast.

"Oh—oh Gray—" I cried, beseeching him. His hips made feathering motions above me, my pussy stretched wide, so sensitive, just about to be set off—"Yes!" I shouted, disturbing a curious flock of birds overhead. "Yes!" I shouted a little more softly, bucking up and around his hard cock, the weight of him catching my thrashing. He growled in satisfaction, I could feel his chest rumble against mine.

"Good," he said approvingly. "My turn now, but don't worry, you'll get more," he promised—and I did.

CHAPTER THIRTEEN
ANGELA

We returned to the bar late that evening. He dropped me off and begged off to go do 'business' and I'd lost the will to fight, he'd fucked it clean away. I'd lost count of the times he'd made me come, and then come in me, his cock solidly inside my pussy the entire time. When he'd finally pulled it out it looked the same—but I knew the weight and girth I'd felt, even if I'd feel foolish trying to explain it away out loud. I tried not to walk like I'd been riding a horse as I went through the crowded bar back to our bedroom.

Willa was dozing on our communal bed. Being pregnant was taking a lot out of her. I tried to be quiet, but she still woke as I snuggled in.

"Is everything okay?" Her hand reached for mine. "I was so worried."

"It's all fine now, I think. He really does love us, Willa. He's just...." Once Gray and I had started fucking we'd stopped talking. But I knew what his body'd said—that he wanted to make things right.

"I know," she said, forgiving my lack of words and squeezing my hand. "I know."

THE NEXT MORNING Gray hadn't come back yet. I was up before Willa, and went to the bathroom to comb my hair and brush my teeth—and saw where my pill pack sat, open, the half-circle of pills at the bottom of it smiling at me.

Shit. I'd been so worried about Willa—and then so thoroughly fucked—that for two days I hadn't taken any. And—worse yet—now I had strange cramps.

There was no way. I couldn't be *that* unlucky, could I?

But after the way Gray had been yesterday—and how Willa was now—I bit my lip—and then I popped out the two pills I'd missed into the toilet. If I was, I was. And if I wasn't—I could be.

I SPENT the next two weeks popping pills out and flushing them. We —all three of us, and variations thereof—fucked again and again, but it never had the same intensity. Gray was more attentive now, to both of us, to be sure—but it never felt so completely right. Although maybe I could blame myself—when my blank week came and my period didn't—I knew I was acting strange. I'd always skipped my periods though, taking my pills sequentially, all the better to keep getting laid. So the only one that knew the difference was me.

I mean, I wanted to tell them, I knew they'd both be happy. But any time I wanted to, something came up—more business, more problems, or more tattoos to do. I found out more gossip from the pack members I gave tattoos to each night than from Gray. School-work got short shrift as I tried to imagine myself pregnant, taking a sweltering bus into campus, or riding at nine months on the back of Gray's bike.

And then came the Farm night.

"Oh my God, Angie," Willa said, wincing in pain. Her face was sallow, she hadn't kept food down in three days. Nikki had brought her over an herbal cocktail of some sort. Willa was sipping on it now when she could, over ice.

I looked over to where Gray sat, lacing his boots up for the ride. I didn't have to say anything for him to know what I was thinking. "It'll pass. It always does."

"How can you be so sure?"

"Because," he said, standing, and coming over to me. He kissed my head, and then he kissed hers, and went for the door.

I lay down beside Willa, swallowing my own queasiness down. My mother had always joked she was made of breeding stock, that her pregnancy had been a pain-free joy, and up until this night I'd been inclined to agree. But something felt wrong now, inside me, in a way that I couldn't describe.

"It's going to be okay, right Angie?" Willa asked, breathing stomach acid out at me.

"Yeah. Of course."

An hour later Murphy knocked on the door. Someone always checked in on us on Farm nights. "You two okay?"

"Yeah," I shouted out.

There was a pause. "You want your shot?"

At the thought of tequila, above and beyond what it might do to my baby, my stomach curdled. "You drink it for me!"

"Suit yourself," he said back, surely slinking away.

I EXPECTED that night to be like all the other Farm nights for Willa—bad but then easing up near dawn.

But that's not what happened. Around midnight, she started weeping, and after that—

"Oh my God," I whispered, and then raced out into the bar. "Someone—help me!"

The bar was mostly empty—on Farm nights, we didn't let outsiders inside. No one seemed particularly moved.

"Willa—she's having a miscarriage!" I rounded the bar to Murphy. "I need you—we've got to take her into the hospital. Now!"

Murphy inhaled deeply, looking sorrowfully at me. "No. We don't," he said, his voice low.

"What? Didn't you hear me? She needs a doctor! She's going to lose the baby!" I'd left my best friend in a slowly growing pool of blood.

"She'll either make it, or she won't," he said. I looked around for someone, anyone, less insane.

"But," I sputtered.

"Go back to the room. See if there's anything you can do to make her more comfortable," he said, his expression turning stony.

I already knew there was nothing I could do for her—she needed medical attention. "You're crazy!" I said, and went for the phone behind the bar.

He caught me just as I reached it, hauling me back by my waist. The strange bottle of whatever they kept back there to add to their shots tipped on the shelf and spattered, and some of the liquid hit his hand. He yanked it back as if it burned and shouted, "Goddammit Angie!" dropping me.

My phone was in the bedroom—but if I went back in there—they'd bar me in and wouldn't let me go for help. I ran for the back patio and the communal car.

CHAPTER FOURTEEN
ANGELA

It was raining outside. One of the torrential rains that happens sometimes in the desert, like the sky's unzipped itself and everything inside of it pours out. I barely had time to throw the car in reverse before Pack members bounded out of the bar at me, but I hadn't turned on my headlights—I careened wildly into the dark, where I hoped they couldn't see me, able to go further, faster, safer in this weather with the car then them on bikes.

At first I thought I'd drive towards civilization—but if I did that, they would see me. They were probably going that way now, hoping to chase after me.

There was only one other place I could go, one other person I could count on for support. Gray. He—he'd said he loved me. Loved us. He wouldn't just let Willa die. I turned on the next road I recognized, and started weaving up the same way he'd taken me on the bike a month earlier.

The road kept going up—I thought I recognized the same trees, but after ten turns in the rain I didn't know anymore—was I being an idiot? Willa was counting on me—

I blindly took another hair-pin turn, waiting for the farmstead she said she'd seen, where all of Gray's stupid business was happening. And that's when I ran into...something.

It'd been running across the road—it clipped the front of the car and gone spinning unto the underbrush. What the hell had it been? A deer? One of the headlights started to flicker, as I screeched to a halt and got out of the car. Rain was still pouring, the trees above only serving to turn individual raindrops into semi-permanent streams. Everything felt impossible. I didn't know what was really happening, or who to believe, or how to help Willa.

I started to cry as—a wolf emerged from the underbrush beside the road.

That's what I'd hit—oh my *God*.

It came out, head low, lips pulled high, nose twitching as it smelled me. I went completely still, too far away from the car to run back to it safely. The wolf padded over, and by the broken light of the moon and a bolt of lightning, I could see a furless scar, running down its front leg.

"Nice doggie," I whispered and it growled, lifting its head—then rose up on its hind-legs. The move was so unfamiliar I was too awestruck to run. Its feet landed almost precisely where my tattoos were, pushing me down on the wet ground. It stood over me, I could both smell and feel the wet weight of its fur, as it looked down at me with golden eyes. It nipped at my neck, and then started snuffling me all over, working its way down my body, growling any time I moved an inch—until it made its way to my crotch, where it caught its teeth into the seam of my jeans and tugged.

"No!" I shouted, shoving it away. It crouched and snarled at me. "Get away!" Spell broken, I started to look around for something I could use to scare it—and saw another shadow racing in.

Another wolf came out of nowhere and bowled the first wolf over. I scrambled to standing, as both of them growled, teeth bared as they circled, looking for an out. The first wolf's scar was starkly apparent—as was the new wolf's gray coloring, like it was made of the moon itself. The first one lunged in, and the second one twisted, going for its neck and—

Lightning flared overhead, the trees rattling with thunder, making everything momentarily bright. Bright enough for me to see how the wolves' shapes flickered, from wolves to men to back again, like a bad strobe. I slapped a hand across my mouth to stop from screaming and ran for the car, leaping in and then driving perilously backwards down mountain roads.

Inside the car, I could scream. "What the fuck!" I shouted, twisting to look back over my shoulder, trying to figure out which way to go without much light behind me. "What the actual fuck?!" I cursed, my mind unable to bend far enough to understand what was happening—why for a moment back there it'd looked like Gray and Wade were fighting in fur-covered bodies.

I made it halfway down—but a mudslide covered the side of the road, and in an effort to avoid it I'd swung wide and—the car went wide and slid off the edge of the road, the rear wheels sinking into mud.

"No. No!" I said, slamming my hand down into the steering wheel. Willa still needed me—and I needed to be the hell off this mountain. I pressed the gas and the back tires spun without purchase. "Fuck!" I shouted, getting out of the car, so cold I was shaking. The mudslide had come down with a torrent of rocks, I could see them casting jagged shadows with my one good headlight.

And then my artistic eyes saw them for what they really were.

Bones.

A field of them. The pieces to at least ten different skeletons, femurs jutting, shards of skulls. I leaned over, trying to puke. Nothing came up, but the feeling of sickness remained.

I went behind the car to where it'd bottomed out. I needed to get it on the road. If I didn't, I'd be trapped here—with all this death.

"Please," I begged anyone, anything that'd listen. "I've got to get out." I set my hands against the trunk and pushed. Club business—

wolves—and dying girls—whatever Gray was doing, whatever the Pack was into—it wasn't right. And if I didn't get away now, I knew I never would. "Come on," I shoved the car, willing it to somehow help. A sudden wind pushed a cloud away, and moonlight shone down from up above. "Come on!"

A surge of strength flowed through me, through every limb the moonlight touched. I felt it like I was being electrocuted, like a full-body shock. And with a wrenching shove I pushed the car six feet forward.

I stood behind it, panting, feeling like a monster. "You're kidding me," I whispered.

Moonlight faded behind another cloud and the strength it'd given me waned. "My God," I whispered, running up to the driver's side—where a skull with some scraps of hair still attached stared up at me from the ground.

It was up to me, to make a choice. I grabbed it, ignoring the way touching it made me want to vomit madly, and put it in the passenger seat.

THE COPS DIDN'T WANT to hear me until I showed them the skull. I'd had forty minutes driving in to make up a lie. It wasn't very good, but a skull was a skull.

"Your...dog brought these in? From the Farm?" The detective I was talking to was African-American, with his hair in a buzz cut, like he'd just gotten out of the marines. The metal his nametag was printed on, on his desk—Paul Derizzio—was so shiny I was sure it was new.

"Yeah. My dog's always digging where he shouldn't be."

"And you're always out walking him in the rain?" he asked, giving me a look.

"Dog's gotta piss, Mister. Rain doesn't make him hold it." It was all I could do not to shake him into believing me. "You should check it out tonight. Before the rest of her washes away, if she's up there."

"Her?"

I shrugged. "Isn't it always girls that go missing in this town?"

He finished bagging the skull and wrote down my fake name along with my fake phone number.

"You should stay here, while we go check it out."

"Fine, but I've got to pee myself," I said.

"It's one door behind you." He pointed back, but his attention was on the skull now, not me. I heard him call for someone else to look as I dodged to sneak out, the thin nightshift crew none the wiser.

AND THEN, I went back to the bar.

I could've, should've run. But I knew I'd seen too much—and done too much, now that I'd talked to the police. There was no way the Pack wouldn't catch me. I knew them, I knew Gray, they could chase anyone down. And now I knew why—chasing must come easy to werewolves.

But you're probably asking yourself why I didn't tell the cops about Willa. I think it was because I knew, somewhere inside me, that it was already too late. The truth about what the Pack was, was settling inside me—just like Gray's child. The monster that he'd put in me, and the monster I'd somehow let myself become.

But Willa? She didn't know. And I knew, on some level, woman to woman, that she wasn't strong enough to make it.

The only thing left to do was to find out for myself. I drove up, the bar denuded of motorcycles, and found Murphy sitting behind the counter, looking grim and nursing his hand.

"You look like shit," I said.

"So do you."

"I got into an accident. I've been in a ditch for three hours—I just got a tow."

His face showed the merest hint of concern. "That explains why the boys couldn't find you."

"Not my proudest night," I said, slicking my wet hair back, praying the rain had washed away any of the smell from the precinct. "How is she?"

He inhaled deeply, to tell me the bad news I could already feel in the air. "She—she didn't make it."

And even though I knew it was coming, it still felt like a blow. "What happened?"

"Her baby...." he said, rounding the bar to my side. "It just—didn't work out in her. It happens sometimes, you know?"

I sank down to my knees. "I wanted to take her in—"

"Doctors couldn't have helped. They don't know everything—"

"They know a fuck more than you do!" I screamed at him. Even though I knew what'd happened—it was still his—Gray's—all the Pack's fault. Even the women that tried to help her. I swooned with the enormity of it—literally every other true pack member was in on it. All of them knew that Willa might die and none of them tried to save her. All to give another baby to the Pack.

The realization broke me and I howled, sobbing.

"I know, girl, I know," Murphy said, patting my back, consolingly.

"You don't know shit," I cried, and sank to all fours.

I cried it out there, on the floor of the bar, and when I could stagger to standing I did so, walking behind the bar.

"What're you getting into?"

"My best friend just died. I need a drink."

Murphy nodded as I pulled out a PBR—and turned the bottle they all added to shots around. The label'd been ripped off, but poorly, and I could make out half a word.

'Ver.'

Sil-*ver*, my brain filled in. *Obviously.*

I took the unopened can back into the bedroom. Willa wasn't there. Neither were the sheets, or the presumably bloody mattress. Just a bed frame and a jumble of our pillows on the floor. I went through them until I found the one that smelled like her and lay down on the ground at the foot of the bed, waiting for Gray to come home and kill me.

CHAPTER FIFTEEN
ANGELA

I don't know how I slept, but I managed to until Gray came home the next morning.

"Oh baby, I heard," he said, coming across the room and sinking to my level, reaching for me.

I—I fought him then—I didn't want him to touch me—but he wasn't trying to hurt me, he was trying to console me, pressing me to his chest as I squirmed until I pushed myself away from him. The sorrow that scored his face—how could he pretend to be upset? He had to know the danger he'd put her in when he gotten her pregnant. More werewolves didn't just come out of a machine.

"I wanted to be here. I would've if I could," he went on, apologizing.

Apologizing!

Like he didn't know what I'd seen! And—maybe he didn't. I'd only seen the wolf part of him, really, on his wild night. Maybe the wolf part didn't talk to him? How could it? It was an animal.

And I miraculously wasn't dead. He didn't even seem interested in killing me. So I doubled down.

"She died. Because of you!" I shouted at him, and started hitting him, beating closed fists on his chest.

"Ang, stop that," he said, catching me.

"They wouldn't let me take her in! And then when I tried to, I got into an accident—and you should've been there!" I said, falling into all too real tears, letting my sorrow break me.

"Shh, sweetheart, shh," he said, pulling me close.

It felt wrong, like a betrayal of all that Willa and I had, letting him touch me anywhere. But if I could manage to live through this, I could live through fucking anything. And I didn't just have myself to live for anymore. I had the baby—that above all else I knew I had to get away from Gray.

The bar's alarm started blaring, warning every one in every room that the police were right outside. Gray scrambled to attention and I followed him up as we heard shouting in the hall. The door to our room kicked open and men with handguns streamed in.

"Erik Bergman, you're under arrest, put your hands up."

Caught unawares, Gray started to spin things, looking at each of them like they were all friends. "Hey, we're cool here," he began.

"Does the name Brittani Jacobs ring a bell?" the lead cop said, as he grabbed for Gray's shoulders.

I gasped. The book I'd seen—the one that was still on Gray's desk —was a gift from Brittani. They'd search here, and find it—and Willa and I had never pulled those old dresses from his closet, choosing instead to keep our own clothing in assorted piles on the floor.

"Who're you?" a detective shouted down at me. I held my hands up.

"She's nobody," Gray said, giving me a look that I knew meant I should keep my mouth shut.

And then the detective I'd met last night came in the room, pulling up the rear. He saw me and I saw the flash of recognition in his eyes—right before they narrowed, taking the situation in.

"I don't know anything," I said. "What the hell is going on, Gray?" I kept making innocent sounds, pleading Detective Derizzio with my eyes—and he, likely pleased to take credit for the first big Pack bust, nodded subtly, knowing anything more than that would condemn me to die.

"Just stay quiet," Gray demanded, as the cops nearest him started shoving him out while reciting Miranda rights.

THE PACK DESCENDED INTO CHAOS.

The cops tossed our room and found Brittani's book and dresses she'd been photographed in. I didn't really have a place to stay there anymore—but I didn't feel like I could go. I was worried abandoning the bar would cast suspicion on myself. I did, however, spend a lot of time moping and crying everywhere—half-fake, half-true.

But after a month, I knew I needed out. Each morning I woke up, worrying I would show. I'd reached out to my folks, I knew they would take me back—and I had to go before pretending to be a devoted girlfriend to a man I hated drove me insane.

So one morning I hitched my backpack over my shoulder and walked out like I was going to the bus stop, even though there wasn't school that day—and that's when I remembered my Dringenbergs from Wade. My parents didn't know about my tattooing and if I told them they'd think it was a fad—they'd never spring to replace five-hundred-plus dollar machines.

I trotted back in like I'd forgotten a book and grabbed them, then went for the front door.

Wade blocked my path. "Where do you think you're going?"

Ever since Gray had been taken, he'd been trying to comfort me. He also clearly remembered nothing about his wolf-night. I regarded him coolly. "Out."

He looked me up and down and took a moment to think for himself, measuring some internal tide. "I don't think so," he said, and grabbed me.

"You put me right down this instant Wade!" I shouted, loud enough for half the mall to hear. "I mean it!"

I started throwing punches, right and left, but anywhere they landed felt like stone—it was like the man had no give to him, and he had little care for me. He hauled me into the bedroom, where I'd made a pallet of Willa and I's clothing where the bed'd been, and threw me onto it.

"Wade, don't you dare," I growled—and felt *her*, for the first time since that night beneath the moonlight. My own wolf, welling up inside me, her fur hidden just under my skin.

He didn't notice the change in me, he was too eager to unlatch his belt. "Take your clothes off or I'll rip them off you."

My wolf wanted no part of this indignity. I had blinding waves of emotions from her—anger, ferocity, so strong they left me reeling.

But if I let her out now—the Pack would claim me. They'd never let me go alive. And if I died—I put a hand on my stomach, where any day my baby—*my* baby, not Gray's—would show.

For my baby's sake, I could swallow my pride.

"Fuck you, Wade," I said, but I shoved my jeans down.

THAT WAS AS MUCH of an invitation as he needed. He didn't take the rest of his clothing off either, he was too excited, with me this close, he had to be inside. He curled beside me, setting his body against mine and I could feel his cock, jutting ramrod straight, begging to get in. He lowered himself, hauling my hips towards his and prying my clenched legs apart with his much stronger hands. Despite my decision to take it and live, my body couldn't help but fight—and he acted like he was used to such things. At any rate, it didn't stop him—and soon his cock was chafing me as it rubbed in, dry.

"Ever since I saw you, Angela—ever since I smelled you—I've wanted this," he growled, one hand holding my leg up and open, the other clutching my shoulder, hauling me back onto him, so that he could thrust while I lay still.

"I never wanted anything to do with you," I hissed.

"That's not true. You liked the attention. You liked sharing my art." Now that he was drilled solidly inside he let my leg down and reached up to grab my hair. "You were special—and now you belong to me."

"I hate you. I've always hated you," I said through gritted teeth.

He laughed. "That's what they all say—at first." Then he rolled himself on top of me.

I buried my face in the clothing at hand, willing myself to leave my body. My body was just a meat-thing, and he could have his way with it, but I was still me. And someday, somehow, I would kill him for this. For Willa, and her baby. I would figure out a way to kill them all.

His hands clawed the ground on either side of my head, and I could see his scar, along with the heart I'd sketched on him over a year ago. "Yes—yes—oh my god—yes," the last word left him as a wild howl and I knew he was coming inside me. I closed my eyes shut. Inside the bar, a wall away, I imagined I could hear smattered applause.

And then his cock in me flared, same as Gray's had, in the woods near the Farm.

"Oh, God—I didn't mean for that to happen—but it feels so right," he said, lowering himself on top of me, crushing me down. "I couldn't help it—you're so hot—the moon's near—and my wolf wants you—needs you—God!" he shouted, rolling himself through another thrust. "You're so goddamned tight, and now your pussy's all mine for the taking," he breathed into my ear, still rocking back and forth, satisfying himself again and again, until I imagined myself overflowing with his cum. "How the hell did Gray resist this? How could he stand not knotting you?"

So that's what it was called. I twisted my head and opened up my eyes a mere sliver. "He didn't."

That gave Wade pause.

"He knotted me—and now I'm pregnant with his baby," I whispered.

Wade tried to pull back, but couldn't, his cock had him trapped inside me.

"I'm not just another fly-by-night hussy to him, Wade. And when he gets out of jail and finds out what you've done," I let the barest hint of my wolf out, letting my voice fill with her threat.

He lifted himself up off my back. "I—I didn't mean to. It was my wolf—I swear it."

"The same wolf you drink silver to keep at bay?" I twisted in time to see him nod. "What happened to Willa? And the other girl?"

He swallowed, I heard it. "Men we can bite in. But women have to make it to term."

I twisted to reach up and touch his throat, his cock still spreading me wide. "Which do you think he'll pull your windpipe out with, Wade? His teeth, or his hand?"

"I could kill you now."

"My parents know I live here. The Pack's already under scrutiny, it'd be too messy. And then the autopsy would show I was pregnant, besides."

"You still might die."

"I might. But I'm going to take my chances in the outside world. And you're going to let me." I kept twisting against him, trying to escape the thick pressure of his cock, like a tail between my legs.

"God—if you don't stop—it'll never go down," he said, looking haunted.

"We could always cut it off," I muttered, and went still. I had dark thoughts about using his cock for myself, cruelly fucking him while he was trapped with the dawning horror of the situation he'd brought on himself—but that wasn't me. And after far, far too long, his knot began to subside, until both of us could escape the other. I scooted as far away from him as I could and hauled up my jeans.

"Why didn't you say anything?" he accused me.

"I didn't want anyone to know."

He grunted. "So what now?"

"I run out the door, and you don't tell a soul."

"And you won't tell Gray about...."

"This? Not if you don't."

Wade frowned in confusion. "But it's his child—you have to tell him."

"Only if I survive. If I don't, you're in the clear."

"And if you do?"

"Then we both pray he's in prison for life, after what he did to Willa."

He weighed the anger in my words as he stood, shoving himself into his jeans and fastening his belt without taking his eyes off me. "You would've made an excellent mate, Angela."

"Shut the hell up," I said, and ran for the door.

CHAPTER SIXTEEN
ANGELA

My parents did take me back. There were a few tense weeks of 'I told you so's', but after they found out I was pregnant and had escaped, their anger faded into a lingering sense of disappointment.

School...dwindled. Between the fear that some member of the Pack would come and haul me away, plus the vast gulf of life experiences that now divided me from my classmates—I didn't seem to have a connection there. To anywhere—or anyone, really. I felt like I was living in a fog and that things only happened to me distantly, like I was always five steps out of sync.

Full moons were awful. I bought a bottle of colloidal silver like the Pack had behind the bar and spent a week staring it down. Would silver have saved Willa? Maybe. Would it've killed her baby? Maybe that, too. If only she'd been given the choice....

But I knew what I was getting into. And—just like I'd told Willa her child was half her own, my baby was half mine too. So I sat down each full moon night and waited, bottle in hand, feeling my wolf roil around inside my body like she was looking for a way out. I couldn't risk changing like Wade and Gray, I didn't want to wake up tomorrow vomiting up a piece of mom or dad. But either I couldn't change into a full wolf all the way, or she and I reached some sort of internal détente, on behalf of our unborn child.

The only thing that kept me sane then, between the loss and the fear, was my art. All the emotions I could never give voice to I drew or painted out. Nothing was safe—cocktail napkins, the walls of my room, the onesies my mother bought for the baby shower I wouldn't let her throw. And in this way everything I touched became a piece of me, until slowly the real world pulled me back inside, as did my baby —after I made sure to have a C-section on a no-moon night.

I started taking silver—and giving it to Rabbit—the day after.

CHAPTER SEVENTEEN
ANGELA

I worked my way up in a shop—a shop that'd only given me a chance to show them my art because of my guns, fuck you again Wade—until I had a regular clientele and the money I brought in was respectable enough for my mom to stop telling me to get a real job. Then my dad died of a heart attack and left enough money behind for my mom to partially stake me starting up Dark Ink.

For the first year it was rocky—no matter how hard I worked, I was always behind on my loans, but after I got enough good artists beneath me, things evened out. I didn't want to call it breathing room, but we had a little space. Enough for me to sort of try to be normal again, which was why I went out on a 'date'—I needed practice at it.

I made it as far as the door of the restaurant where I was supposed to meet some guy. We'd chatted online and he didn't seem like a serial killer—but seeing as I'd had vastly poor taste in men before, I hadn't taken any silver today, just in case I needed to bring my wolf to bear. I knew that if I needed her, she'd make me strong enough to take any man.

My mom was home with Rabbit and I was wearing a cute flouncy dress—I hovered outside the restaurant's door, looking at myself in the glass. Who was I fooling? This wasn't me. I couldn't let my guard down. Not ever again. I turned away, feeling my wolf growl inside me, in deep disappointment at her fragile human shell. She wanted out—she wanted a chance to play—whenever I skipped taking silver, *she* was there, hungry to run, to chase, to fuck.

Maybe because of her—or maybe to prove to her that I was in charge and could deny her even without silver onboard—I detoured to a bar on the way home. I hadn't set foot in one since the last time I'd left Gray's.

I WENT IN, ordered a beer, and sat down at a high table by my lonesome, taking everything in—and then pulled my phone out, pretending to be waiting for someone, counting down the seconds until I could claim some strange triumph over my past. Everyone in the bar ignored me—except for one good-looking man. I looked up, saw him staring at me for a moment, and then he pulled out a pen.

Oh God. I'd forgotten this was what it was like to be a woman in the world at large. He was writing on something—likely his phone number, likely to give to me. When he pulled away from the bar to walk toward me, bringing a napkin with him, I winced.

"Hey. I know this is weird—but I just saw you and," he shrugged, handing a sketched on cocktail napkin over with a tattooed hand.

What I assumed would be digits or a hand-drawn dick pic was a portrait instead. Of me.

"Thanks," I said, taking it. It was surprisingly well done for being in pen on a napkin and so quickly drawn. "Do things like these get you a lot of play?"

He smiled. "Sometimes. But I tend to only draw really beautiful women, which lowers my average."

I laughed. I was surprised to hear it, it'd been so long. He had full lips, dramatic cheekbones, and expressive dark brown eyes. His body was leanly muscled and tattoos covered both of his hands. It was those that drew me in, they were covered in an ornate designs, well done despite the difficulty that came from tattooing thinner skin.

They were the kind of hands that—attached to the right man—it was hard not to imagine wanting on me.

"I'm Jack," he said, oblivious to my thoughts.

"Angela."

"May I?" he asked, gesturing to my table's empty chair.

"Only if you give me your pen."

He handed his pen over to me, mystified, and pulled his new chair closer to watch me.

I had a finer tipped pen in my purse, but pulling it out might have constituted cheating. I took the portrait he'd made of me and put it on its side and covered it up, turning my profile into the ridge of a mountain, my hair into a stream, and when I handed it back over to him with his pen, he was grinning.

"That was awesome," he said, recreasing the napkin's folds with a finger.

"Thank you."

"You're clearly an artist—please tell me it's more than a hobby."

"It is," I said, and started talking.

WITHIN MINUTES I found out we knew some of the same people, and that Jack was currently freelancing, using other people's studios part-time. He had an easy going manner, sincere, even though he always sounded like he was one sentence away from telling a joke. When he did make jokes, they were often at his own expense, self-deprecating in a wry fashion that wasn't looking for sympathy.

I slowly finished my beer as we chatted and I realized this was far better than any date at that restaurant could've possibly been.

"So, uh," he said, looking between me and my beer. "Do you

want another one? Not that I want to get you drunk, but I do want to keep you here."

His honesty was like a bolt of lightning. It'd been so long since I'd felt like myself I wasn't even sure who I really was—except that I was feeling like her again around him, and my wolf agreed.

"Let's go outside," I said.

One of his eyebrows rose. "Sure," he said, and followed me out.

Two steps out into the night air and I was mauling him. My wolf wanted this—and so did I. I hadn't been with anyone since Willa and Gray, it'd been a long and lonely few years, but kissing him felt right and my intensity didn't scare him. We moved through the parking lot like we were dancing, kissing voraciously and then coming up for air. His mouth fit mine like it was meant for me, our tongues pushed and twined, and every so often he would pull back while biting on my lip, leaving me breathless. He spun us around until my back was against a black vintage car.

"Careful," I said with a laugh as he pressed me against it.

"It's mine—and trust me, I don't care."

My hands were on his chest and his hands were in my hair and we were both taking a moment to reassess and breathe, trying to read each other's eyes. The night was young.

What would we do with the rest of it?

"Do you want to," he began.

I said, "We could..." at the same time.

Then he laughed and I laughed and—in an instant *she* was there. Surging forward, filling me. I looked up—the moon wasn't full yet, but I hadn't taken any silver today, all the better to fight off my theoretical serial killer internet date.

If I thought my genie was bad—she was *hungry*, and she *wanted* him.

"I...." I began, pulling back, pushing *her* down, dropping my hands and shaking my head.

"What?" he gently asked. Sensing the change, he pulled back too.

"I'm a mom, this isn't what moms do," I lied, side-stepping away.

"You sure about that?" he asked with a wicked grin. "I feel like I've probably slept with more moms than you have."

I gave a nervous laugh. "I'm sure."

"Okay," he said, nodding to accept his defeat. "For...tonight? Or for forever?"

"For a really long time that I'm not sure about yet." I brought my hands up. "I'm rusty, and—"

He smiled at me. "You don't have to explain. It's all right. You do what you have to do."

There were a lot of tones his voice could have taken: anger, condescension, disappointment but his was genuine, and I deflated in its sincerity. "Thank you."

"Of course." He jerked his chin at the bar behind us. "Did you want to go back and keep talking?"

I did, *but*. "I probably shouldn't—" More talking would only lead to trouble.

"Sure. I get it," he said. This was not at all how I'd imagined my evening going—him either, from the look he was giving me before he spoke. "This is going to sound awful, but, if this isn't happening—I should probably go finish a friend's sleeve like I was supposed to. You were—and *are*—totally worth standing him up for, even just to hang, but rent's coming up. But I can give you a ride home if you need it, you're tiny, and one beer—"

"No, I'm safe to drive." I shook my head. "But do you always tattoo so late?"

"Yeah. I'm up till dawn, most nights." He gave me a half-smile. "I don't suppose I can get your number?"

I couldn't blame him for trying—hell, I wanted him to try. He was hot, and he would be easy, I could tell. He was the kind of guy who was who he seemed to be on the surface. No tricks—not like me.

Too bad I wasn't ready for this yet. I might be in time, but not tonight—and not while *she* was this hungry.

Or was a little of that me?

"No." I shook my head, while smiling at him regretfully. "But," I said, popping open my purse to pull out a Dark Ink business card, "You can call me here."

He chuckled. "Thanks, but I have my own friends to give me tats."

"No—I'm offering you a job."

"Yeah?" Confusion clouded his face.

"Yeah," I said, strongly nodding. "It's hard to find good vampires."

He startled at that. "What?"

"You know—people willing to stay up till dawn. Good night artists are hard to find." The expression on his face was hard to read, so I pressed on. "This way you could have your own station—you wouldn't have to share anymore. And I take a smaller cut of night-time stations, since it's harder to get walk-in clientele. So I could be good for you—and you could be good for me," I said, and then shut up before I could say anything else embarrassing.

He looked between me and the card. "I see."

"Just think about it? And if you want it, give me a call."

Jack gave me a grin, before making the card dance over his fingers like a coin and putting it in his back pocket. "Definitely."

CHAPTER EIGHTEEN
JACK

"Good morning, sunshine," crooned a familiar French accent as I lurched awake. Rosalie was looming over me in a low-cut dress that hung freely enough for me to see she wasn't wearing a bra. I was on a couch and there was clothing strewn on top of me—and a sense that something horrible had happened, to me and to—

"Thea?"

Rosalie rocked back, her disappointment obvious. "Yes, her, of course."

I sat up, knocking a wave of fabric off, realizing I was naked in time to hide myself with a corset. I felt hungover, terrified, and I was starving. "What happened?" The last thing I remembered—it couldn't have been true—and yet here I was.

"I promised I'd tell you who took Thea, and where, if you gave yourself to me. Which you, passionately in love with your girlfriend, did." The way Rosalie said the word girlfriend made it drip with irony. "So now you are mine."

"What? Where are my clothes? Where is she?"

"Everything in good time, *mon ami*. You can't just go on without knowing the rules. Otherwise you'll die and be no good to us both."

Whatever fear I'd felt of Rosalie when I'd last seen her—I didn't feel it now. I grabbed her shoulders. "Whatever you're going to tell me, tell me, but give me my clothing and hurry the fuck up."

"Fine," she said, angling her chin up defiantly. "Are you hungry now, *mon amour*?"

"What does that have to do with anything?"

"*Answer me*," she snapped, and I felt a sudden willingness to obey. I put a hand to my stomach. It felt like my whole body was starving, each and every cell.

"I am."

"That's the hunger. You were out for three days, becoming what you now are. If you try to ignore it, it will only get worse."

"'What you now are'," I snarled back at her. "What the hell do you mean?"

She studied me intently. "Sometimes people remember. Sometimes they don't." Then she opened her mouth wide and let me see needle-like teeth sinking down from just behind her own.

My own jaw dropped, in horror. I did remember, seeing those teeth lower into me and—I reached for my neck.

"You do remember," she said with a laugh.

I scanned the room wildly for an exit. She was small, I could take her—I could beat her to the door.

"*No running*," she commanded, and suddenly escape was not an option as I was, once again, glued to her couch.

These were no hypnotist's tricks. "What are you?"

"That's the wrong question, Jack. You should be asking, 'What are we?'" She gestured between us both. "Thea's other boyfriend is a lieutenant in the Nevada 13, who considered himself a bit of a ladies man. Then when he found out she was fucking you on the side...."

The full extent of what she'd said hit home. "Three days? I've been out for three days?" I tried again to move, but couldn't.

"In the service of a larger cause! You wanted to be strong enough to fight him. You couldn't before—but now you can. You can take on an army now, Jack." She grabbed hold of my bicep and squeezed.

I did feel stronger...but....

"You just need to eat. And then you can be on your way. I'll have Tamo drop you off—he'll even wait for you outside."

I did need to eat. Hunger pangs wracked through me. Then I remembered her fangs—and her implication that I had them, too. I searched behind my teeth for them with my tongue before asking, "Eat...what?"

A slow smile spread across her face, revealing a row of even teeth, no fangs in sight. "Only two ways to satisfy it. I can bring a girl in for you to bite—or you can give me a good fuck."

"You have to be kidding on both counts. I'm not biting anyone—and I wouldn't fuck you with someone else's dick." I struggled against muscles that wouldn't obey. "Let me go, and I can manage on my own."

"You're a vampire now, Jack. One of the divine undead. For the entire rest of your time on this planet you'll be foraging for life, one way or another." She rose and crossed the room to knock on her door, then spoke briefly to someone outside.

She waited until the door opened again from the other side and reached out, hauling a girl with fire-engine red hair I didn't recognize in. Rosalie practically threw her to the floor at my feet. She spilled down, all gawky legs and arms, breasts free and jiggling, the lower half of a sexy Little Bo Peep outfit completing her terrified look.

"Who is he, Miss Rosalie?" she asked in all innocence, from the floor.

She addressed me, instead. "There. If you won't fuck me, fuck her."

"I will not."

"Then bite her."

"I won't do that, either!" Rage built in me, over what'd happened to me, what was likely happening to Thea, over three wasted days—and I used it to pry myself off the couch, just barely managing to stand.

The girl on the floor's eyes went wide just as Rosalie clapped her hands. "Impressive! But I had a feeling you would be." She snapped, and the command I was fighting released, making me sag forward. The girl on the floor scooted back quickly with a gasp, and my eyes were drawn to her instantly. She looked the very picture of innocence, delicious in so many dangerous ways. Her lips parted as she continued to pant in fear—and I felt like I could see the blood in her —but that was impossible. I shook my head to clear it.

Rosalie came to stand between us and put her hand on my jaw. "You can't fight for Thea in your current state and you know that. You'll go mad between now and then and kill the first tourist you see. So just eat the bird I've given you, rather than slaughtering two in the bush later, no? Save all your killing for Nevadas one through thirteen." She stroked her hand off my chin, then bopped me on the nose with her forefinger. "Don't make me make you fuck her, Jack."

I turned towards her. "You can't. I'm not like you."

Her eyes flashed. "Oh? And just what do you think I am?"

The girl moved again, distracting me. "It's...it's okay." She crawled over on her hands and knees, the costume's broad tutu spiking out in all directions, revealing the heart-shaped curve of her ass under a thong and tights. "See?" she said, coming up to kneel at my feet, reaching for me.

My body—reacted. Not just my cock, the omnipresent male hunger than every man knew—but something deeper, more frightening and wilder. It knew what she was offering, and it wanted to take it.

She angled up like a stretching cat and put a hand on both my thighs. Her lips parted and my cock rose up to meet them, and when she leaned forward, taking my head into her mouth it felt like I was entering something holy.

"Oh—my God," I whispered, transfixed by the sensation.

Rosalie purred. "It's not always like that. But when it is, it's nice." She brought a handful of nails clawing down my back.

The woman's heavily lined eyes looked up, searching mine for some sign of satisfaction. I brought both hands to her hair and gently thrust, making her mouth take more of me, watching my cock thread the red ribbon of her lips.

I felt the slimmest edge of hunger recede, at last—so that hadn't been a lie. "What is this?" I asked, watching the woman work her way down my cock, equally ecstatic and mystified.

"It's life. Sex is its own kind of magic—power, intention, fluids—all mixed into one. Blood's good too, and quicker generally, but," she stroked her fingers through the girl's hair, as she started to earnestly take me, bobbing on and off of me, making the head of my cock dive down the back of her throat. "If you don't want to leave a string of bodies, this is better. When it's done right, of course."

I moaned, some part of me knowing I was betraying Thea, but the rest of me completely unable to resist this—it was like with each stroke she was pulling the hunger itself out of me as she sucked on my cock.

Then she pulled back entirely, sinking onto her heels, just as I thought my cock might burst. In a movement more fluid than I would've given her credit for, she turned, showing me everything the tutu hid.

I—I needed more—*but Thea*—

She looked forlornly over her shoulder at me, casting a lock of red hair back. "Don't you want me?" she asked, her voice seemingly sincere and—

I fell to my knees, ripping through her tights, yanking her thong aside. Her pussy underneath was already wet, which was good because I needed to be inside it. I spread her wide with my hands and buried myself deep.

She let out a cry of surprise, but I felt her twitch around me as if to hold me there—and then I realized—

"I'm sorry—condoms," I started trying to back out, only to find Rosalie at my back.

"You're already dead. What on earth could you need a condom for?"

The red-head didn't seem put off by her strange pronouncement —in fact she'd started rocking back and forth. And I—I grabbed beneath the tulle to pull her hips to me.

What happened next, was wild, savage. I took her, bending myself over her, grabbing her shoulders, hips, hair, anything I could to make her mate with me. As much hunger as she'd taken away was as much empty space I had to fill.

She cried out, bracing against the ground to take more of me. "Oh—fuck me!" she shouted, a command, not an exclamation. I redoubled my efforts, impossibly, and felt her pussy start to squeeze.

"Yes—yes—get me off—I need it—get me off!" she pleaded, her hands clenching into fists against the ground.

"I—I—" I panted, fucking her madly, feeling like my own cock was about to explode—I reached under to grab her breasts and drove my cock deep. "Come," I growled, from someplace deep inside.

She stiffened under me and around me.

"*Come*," I commanded, with the strange skill of Rosalie.

Her body started shuddering beneath me. "Oh, yes, Daddy!" and then she let out a high pitched squeal.

Her orgasm milked me dry. It'd been so long since I'd been in a woman, condom-free, feeling her pussy pulse felt like the essence of luxury. I felt myself spurting into her, my hips spasming on their own as I grunted above. I kept fucking her until I was through, until her pussy had eaten every last drop, and then pulled back slowly, drawing out the feel.

The red-head sagged forward, collapsing into a heap of tulle, legs splayed so I could see my cum leaking out through her swollen pink lips.

"Was that good for you, darling?" Rosalie asked. It took me a moment to realize she was talking to the girl.

"Uh-huh." The red-head nodded, coming up onto her elbows. "For a night or two. Or three." She rolled over onto her back and laughed, pushing a hand down between her legs to rub her clit. "And much better than the alternative."

"Did you really think that I would let him bleed you?"

"It would be no fair if I didn't get to bleed him back."

"He needs all his blood inside him, for now." Rosalie chuckled and then looked over. "And you?"

I didn't understand what was happening but, "I feel—better."

"Don't get too used to it. It won't last for long—but it will last for long enough."

I looked down at myself—I should've at least felt drained, or sore, but instead I felt—revitalized. "I have to fuck...every night? Like that?"

"Maybe not so much like that. I think if Maya were a normal girl, you might have killed her."

"He wasn't that good." The red-head, Maya, rolled her eyes. "I liked fucking him better when he was comatose. Less talking, more cocking."

"Wait...." I crawled backwards in horror as what she said sunk in and Maya laughed. "You—is everyone here a...."

"You can just say it. A vampire." Rosalie put the word to it at last, as she reached into her closet. "And no. Only two or three."

"Thea?" If she were, it'd explain the sex we'd been having.

"Of course not, otherwise I wouldn't be needing to send you after her."

"I—I still don't understand."

"You're going to go out with Tamo," she said, throwing jeans and a t-shirt at me followed by my own old boots.

"If you're a vampire, why didn't you go after her?" I started hauling clothes on.

"Because people have eyes. They can see me. I'm well known. Whereas you? You're a nobody. Tamo knows where to go. He'll bring you back before dawn, assuming you survive."

"How immortal am I?"

"Quite. But watch out for rogue decapitations. Can't survive that."

"Crosses, garlic, mirrors?"

"Stay away from all night wedding chapels and Italian restaurants." And then she gestured at herself in her own mirror, by way of example. "And," she went on, "remember that you owe me."

I had a feeling she wasn't being metaphorical. "How much...and of what?"

"Money or blood. Don't worry—we'll figure out a payment plan." She gave me a winning smile and I left the room carefully, unwilling to turn my back on her.

CHAPTER NINETEEN
JACK

Five minutes later I was sitting in a car with a taciturn Tamo, him driving us off to who knew where.

"Are you...?" I let my voice drift, wondering if the huge man was like me.

"No."

"Why didn't you stop him when you had the chance?" I asked at a red light.

"I'm a lover not a fighter," he said, leering over and daring me to contradict him.

I clenched my hands into unsure fists, like I was going to punch the air. "Do you have any advice? Or guns?"

"Neither. But you'll be fine."

"How do you know?"

"I've seen things like this go down before." He took a wide right hand turn, and took me to what I was sure was the seedier side of town.

The block we wound up on had a series of huge warehouses, all of them unmarked. He cut his headlights and engine and glided to a stop in neutral like someone who'd done this before.

"She's in there. With the rest of them. The entrance is around the back."

"How many?"

"I don't know."

"What happens if I get shot or knifed?"

He hit the unlock button on his door. "You'll see."

Uncertain of anything but my need to save Thea, I got out of the car.

I SNUCK around the building's perimeter. During my brief time on the streets, I'd learned how to skulk—it wasn't always that you were up to no good, sometimes you just didn't need the wrong kind of attention. Walking boldly on sidewalks under streetlights was the kind of thing people who had homes got to do.

But this was slightly different. I felt like the dark welcomed me. I wasn't in any danger of stepping on boards with nails, despite the omnipresent rubble—it was like even in sheer darkness I had a beam of moonlight guiding me, though when I looked up there was no moon to be seen.

And—I could smell things. I scented the strong cologne of the man guarding the door downwind. I heard his voice too, so clear it was like he was talking to me—but it was an argument, on his phone, with a girlfriend.

All in all, he wasn't much of a guard.

Just like I wasn't much of a vampire—yet.

But trusting in this new and untested part of me, I snuck as close as I could, coming in behind him and then—I snapped his neck. Completely naturally.

One moment he was talking, the next I reached out and clapped hands on head and jaw, and then a sound like the crack of a falling tree. He crumpled, his phone dropping as he did, leaving his girlfriend to shout at the pavement. I stepped back into the shadows and if I had had anything in my stomach, I would've barfed it up.

I'd fought before—but I'd never killed anyone. I couldn't believe I had now—whoever'd done that, couldn't have been me. But there the man was, at my feet, not breathing, his eyes staring blankly. I stood, shaking all over in horrified disbelief as the door behind me opened, and caught on the fallen guard's calf.

"What the," I heard the man inside exclaim. The air that came out with him had a strong scent of nail polish mixed with gasoline— what I knew to be the scent of cocaine—and one tiny note of musk from Thea.

And that was that. Whatever I'd done—whatever I was about to do—all could be forgiven.

I slammed the door back into his face, heard it smack him silly and him stumble to the ground. I opened the door up and walked in, kicking him, watching him skid across a cement floored hallway. It felt like I was watching violence on TV, it couldn't have been me doing it, no matter that I was.

"Hey!" shouted someone else as they ran in, reaching for a gun. I ignored it and ran for him—faster than I'd ever ran before. I reached him before he'd unholstered it fully and tackled him, taking him down, then pulling the gun out to bludgeon him with it.

From behind me, I heard a gun cock, and whirled, shooting at the new stranger. My aim was instinctive and amazing—the bullet went right between his eyes and dropped him. Red welled out of the hole, and something inside me churned eagerly. *Blood.* Horrified, I threw away the gun—just as another three men ran in.

After that, it was almost like a video game. Waves of angry men, brutal fighting, and then room after room cleared as they fell, half of them broken, half of them worse. I made my way into the center of the building, past frightened people screaming, naked and chained to desks, packaging up kilos of cocaine into smaller bags. I ignored them for now, I'd free them later, but first I had to find Thea—

I heard a muffled scream behind a door. I whirled on it and

kicked it open, making it swing on its hinges, and heard a man shout in surprise inside.

"Who the hell are you?" It was King Kong. Behind him, Thea was chained, just like the workers outside—and he was trying to protect her. From me.

He didn't wait for an answer. Bullets pummeled my chest. I felt the way they disrupted me as they passed through, churning organs that had each had their use in the mortal world, but now? I didn't know. He emptied his clip, some of his shots going wide in his terror, all the while Thea screamed behind him.

I looked down and saw blood, my blood, well out of five separate holes. It seemed like both a fantastic waste and an invasion of my privacy. My blood was *mine*—and all blood belonged to *me*. I had caused so much carnage and ignored it all—not anymore. Fangs tore through the palate of my mouth at the ready.

"What the fuck are you, man?" he shouted, his voice rising in terror.

It was too hard to talk with fangs down—plus I didn't have an answer for him. I just let the hunger take me.

CHAPTER TWENTY
JACK

The next thing I remembered, I was painted in his blood. Thea was curled into a ball, facing away from me, saying, "Oh-my-God, oh-my-God, oh-my-God," in a chant.

Light-pink intestines were mazed upon the floor and his ribs jutted up at unnatural angles. Gauzy deflated lungs were torn on either side, and I—I looked down. I was holding his heart. I'd torn it open to drink the sweet blood inside like it was a melon.

"Oh, God," I said, just like Thea.

She dared a glance at me. "Jack? Is that you?" Her voice was so quiet in her terror even I could barely hear.

"I'm not sure." As the darkness faded and more of me came back —I could feel all the places my shirt stuck to me with drying gore.

She twisted toward me. Her blonde hair was greasy and she'd never gotten to wash all her make-up from the club off. "Jack—what happened?"

"I had to save you." I opened up my hand and the wet remnants of his heart fell to the cement with a squelch. I reached for her with my bloody hand and she pulled back, hugging the wall. "I didn't mean for this to happen though." No wonder Rosalie hadn't been worried about me surviving, or Tamo. "Are you okay?" I asked, leaving my hand out but not coming closer.

Thea put her free hand to her mouth. "I don't know. I think so. Are...you?"

I stared at the heart where I'd dropped it. "No." I didn't know if I'd ever be okay again.

"How did you do all this? I saw him shoot you—and what was with all the eating?" her voice rising as she panicked.

I opened my mouth to tell her—and then realized the less she knew, the better. The gulf that there'd always been between us had just widened to an impossible extent—the very difference between life and death.

She took my silence for disapproval. "I didn't love him, Jack. Rosalie made me dance for him. I wanted to stop, but every time he came into the club she made me and—at night it somehow made sense, but in the mornings? I didn't know what to do. It was like I was his girlfriend, but I didn't want to be, I swear, she made me. I know that sounds crazy—but you don't know how she can be."

"I believe you."

She unspooled herself toward me as far as she could come with the chain. "I never wanted you to know. I didn't want you to be disappointed in me. What we had—I wanted to have it for forever. Just you and me." She reached toward me with a fluttering hand.

I stepped past her, ignoring it, reaching for the chain against the wall. With a strong tug it came free and she crawled forward through the gore, finding a set of keys in her dead captor's pocket.

"Glad I didn't swallow those," I said, watching her undo a padlock.

"Me too," she said grimly, scooting back to stand more than an arm's length away. She was still wearing what she'd been taken from the club in, minus her heels, and she looked shaken and scared, like the girl I'd pulled from the wreckage once again.

"Why do you always need saving?" I whispered, and she heard.

"Jack—I," she licked her lips and took a step forward.

"Stop right there," I said, and she did, swallowing the words. "Because I'm going to imagine for the rest of my life that you were going to tell me 'I love you'. If you weren't—I don't want to know better. And if you were, hearing it now would break me."

She bit her lips and nodded, as tears welled in her eyes.

"You need to go, Thea. Vegas isn't safe for you." Who knew how many of the girls in Rosalie's employee were being used like this, to further Rosalie's private aims? I couldn't let her go back there.

"To where?"

"On that trip around the world." I leaned over and grabbed the dead man's wallet. It was stuffed with hundreds. "Is there another way out of here?" If there wasn't I would make one.

"I think so—I think his car is parked in the front." She held up the keys.

"Good. Take it—jump the curb until you hit the road—do not go back that way, okay?" I pointed to where I'd come in, at the back of the warehouse. Everything would be over if Tamo saw her. "Grab someone's coat, pants, whatever you need, and get to a hotel till dawn. Clean yourself up there—but do not go to sleep, and do not go home till daylight. After that, grab your passport and luggage, and go. Don't talk to anyone. Get to the airport and start flying—and don't stop until you're in a different country."

She looked so confused and everything in me wanted to hold her. "But what about you?" she asked.

"I'm going to go back to the club and tell Rosalie you died."

She took a step nearer me. "She'll know you're lying—she always does."

"Not until it's too late."

Thea looked stricken. "Come with me, Jack. I—I need you. I always have, I was just so stubborn—"

I wanted to kiss her, but my mouth tasted like another man's blood. "I can't."

"But—"

"Go. Remember—hide until dawn."

She teetered in place like she was still wearing high heels. "Jack —I'm so sorry—"

"Me too." I could write a book about all the ways I was sorry now —and her hand reached back out. If I let her touch me—if all of this was for nothing—"*Go!*" I shouted at her, and she leapt back as though I'd burned her. Her eyes widened—and then she ran for the door.

CHAPTER TWENTY-ONE
JACK

I heard her scurrying away behind me as I returned to the room full of traumatized gang 'workers'. They started screaming, which I ignored, and I pulled up the ends of their chains like popping drain plugs out of so many old fashioned tubs. They, in their wisdom, started running out the door with bricks of coke. I wasn't inclined to stop them. I waited until they'd cleared out, hopefully distracting Tamo from the sounds of Thea's car, as I walked back to pick up the padlock, chain, and cuff she'd dropped, pocketing the still open padlock and winding the chain around my arm like a trophy.

Tamo was still sitting outside in his car as I walked over, unfazed at the blood-covered sight of me. I had a feeling he'd seen worse. "Took you long enough. Where's the girl?"

I stared grimly forward as I got in.

"Like that, eh?" Tamo said.

"You had three fucking days," I muttered.

"Yeah, but I can't take bullets," he said, turning on the engine and putting the car in drive.

"This was never about Thea, was it?"

"Too bad you had to be dead to get smart."

I remembered the way we'd taken to get here from the club—we were taking the reverse commute now, same roads, so I knew where we were. "So how does this work?"

"Guys come to Rosalie when they need help with certain...problems. She's a helpful woman, for the right price."

"So she sold Thea to that guy?"

Tamo glanced over. "Selling's a strong word. She encouraged his natural attraction to her, was all—and her natural attraction to his money."

"Seeing as Rosalie raped me, I don't think selling's too strong." I hadn't put a word to it until that moment, but that'd been what it was.

"Suit yourself." The big man shrugged. "Some other gang was willing to pay for that gang to be broken up, and you were the timely muscle to do it."

"Why not you?"

"Someone trustworthy needs to be around during daylight, to keep the lights on." He accelerated past a stoplight and I saw my moment.

"Funny you should say that," I said. I felt a whole body need to go back to Rosalie—but that didn't stop me from grabbing the steering wheel and yanking it far right. The car reeled sideways, tumbling over an embankment, Tamo and I both bouncing around inside like rocks. I recovered faster, yanking the padlock out of my pocket and the chain off my arm. Tamo pushed himself back off the steering wheel, reeling. There was a jagged cut over his eye, pouring blood. His face went red with frightening anger.

"What the fuck?! I'm gonna," he threatened.

"Lights off," I said, punching him out. I shucked him out of his suit jacket, before chaining his wrist to the wheel, took his phone, wallet, and ran.

. . .

I PULLED on Tamo's jacket to hide the blood on my body. If TVs and movies had taught me anything, it was this: I needed to find a safe place to sleep before dawn. But where could you count on being in the dark all day in Vegas? I then thought about burrowing into the depths of a decrepit casino and stationing myself in front of a slot machine—I wondered how long it'd take them to realize I was dead. But that wasn't really an option—I started walking toward the Strip, thinking I'd find some sort of safe sewer or gutter in a parking garage.

Before I got too far I heard the sound of brakes behind me and a slamming car door. I whirled and saw Rosalie stalking forward out of a car, all done up and angry.

"Where is Tamo?"

"I'm not going back." I knew it as I said the words. I'd let the dawn take me first.

"Your chances of going anywhere are entirely dependent on whether Tamo's still alive."

"I left him breathing." Her eyes narrowed, as she considered whether I told her the truth. "How did you find me?"

"The downside of being my creation is that I always know exactly where you are. And you may not have noticed it, but Vegas is rife with cabs."

"I'm not going back," I repeated, glancing past her to her cabbie, trying to figure out if he'd been compelled to stay or if she'd just told him to leave the meter on.

"What happened?"

I snorted, opening Tamo's huge jacket to show her all of myself, covered in gore. "Exactly what you wanted to happen."

"And the man that took Thea?"

"They'll have to use a shovel to scrape him together for a funeral."

At that, she visibly relaxed. "Good. And the girl?"

"Dead," I lied, just to see if I could.

Her lips pursed and an eyebrow rose. "*Tell me*," she whispered, and the words wound around my heart like a snake and pulled.

I used as few words as I could. "Running away."

Rosalie chuckled at this, walking nearer. "From me? Or from you?"

I followed her with my eyes, trying to betray nothing. "You knew I was going to do that, didn't you. You—cultivated Thea. You cultivated me."

"Don't feel so bad. If it hadn't been you, I would've found someone else suited for the job. And don't worry—I didn't have to push her to be with you—much."

She stood still and watched her words hit me like blows. She was implying that she'd told Thea to take up with me, for the sole purpose of using me later. "Is that true?"

Rosalie gave me a chilling smile. "I guess we'll never know."

I couldn't believe that what I'd shared with Thea was a lie—but the fear of it lodged inside me like a splinter.

"*Come home, Jack,*" Rosalie crooned. My body wanted to obey her, I felt the need surge within, but fought it, barely managing to stay standing. Her eyes widened, then she tsked. "You're a proud man, Jack, I get that. But it's not safe out here for you. You don't know what you're doing, you have no connections and nowhere to go."

"I'd rather die than go back with you."

"I'd rather you didn't—you still owe me, and piles of ash can't make good."

"I owe you?" I let my voice rise in anger. "I just murdered thirty guys for you—you've taken my girlfriend and my life. What more can you possibly want?"

Her eyes searched me as if looking for answers. "All in good time. If you survive long enough, I'll find you. If Tamo doesn't find you first, that is. I won't tell him unless you cross me, but I can't control what he does during the day when I am sleeping. He'll be looking for you now, and if he ever finds out where you sleep...." She drew an elegant finger across her neck and then turned on her heel, stalking back toward her ride. "Good luck, Jack. You'll need it," she said without turning around and got in, closing the door.

I watched her drive away—her cab had one of those fins on top of it for advertisements. *Can you Survive the Night?* shouted in a spooky font, with hordes of undead clawing in from the edges— some sort of zombie survival game, just another way for Vegas to shake money out of tourists.

And....

I walked out onto the next major street and held up a hand. A cab wheeled around for me, no one there to mind a U-turn this late at night. I leaned in. "Hey—you know where that zombie show is? I'm auditioning after-hours—"

"Is any of that shit going to stain my cab?"

"I don't think so." I looked in Tamo's wallet. "There's an extra twenty in it for you, if you get me there by four."

The cabbie appraised me then shrugged. "Sure. Hop in." After I got my seatbelt buckled, he looked back at me in the rearview mirror, rolling down my window remotely. "You stink. Method acting?"

"Something like that," I said.

IT WASN'T hard to jump the fence to get into the back of the zombie game's backlot and, once inside, mingle. The crew of actors moved in a coordinated way around a decorated set—I moved with them. There were zombie victims laying around in assorted rooms as props —when I saw an opportunity I took it, laying down and closing my eyes, listening to the groans of the 'undead' and the next group of victim's earnest screams.

Unlike any of them, I knew what dying felt like—and that screams weren't enough to hold it back. Inside the dark and air conditioned room, I felt dawn rise outside and a weight press down, all my limbs chilling one by one, until the death reached my waist, torso, head. The last thing I heard was: "Wow—that new one looks pretty real."

CHAPTER TWENTY-TWO
JACK

I woke up on a cement floor, stiff and cold, as a group of terrified tourists screamed past—I thought at first by my reanimation, but then realized they were being herded by shuffling actors. I waited until the wave passed and then stood up.

Someone had taken Tamo's jacket—I guess it didn't match the room's décor—but I was otherwise unmolested. I still had his wallet in my back pocket. I didn't dare use the cards but there was a few hundred bucks inside. I wandered back the way I'd come in, past the locker room for the actors, and busted locks open until I found clothes that would fit. I was changing into someone else's jeans when a woman walked in.

"Hey—who're you?"

"A new guy." I could tell my answer didn't pass muster, as she inhaled to scream.

"*Don't*," I commanded her, and her jaw slammed shut. But a second later she looked ready to scream again. So whatever Rosalie did, I could do too—just not as well, or for as long.

"*You didn't see me. I'm gone.*" I said, with more authority. She blinked as though blinded and took a step back. I didn't wait around.

I MADE IT OUTSIDE. I still stunk but at least my clothes weren't dropping scabs. I couldn't risk another night at the zombie shelter after that woman'd seen me, I'd have to find another place to lay low by dawn. I caught a cab, paid him to wait while I went through a drug store and got enough trial sizes to make it through a decent shower, then had him take me to one of the fleabag motels on the outside of town to book a night.

"Skin condition," I told the man behind the counter, as he looked at me. I knew I was still stained with patches of dried blood—I'd seen myself in the mirror of the sunglass stand at the drug store.

"ID?" he asked.

I patted my pockets. My wallet was another thing Rosalie'd claimed.

"I need to see ID," he said more sternly.

"*No you don't.*" I said firmly. The man seemed stunned for a moment, but then processed my cash and gave me a key.

I WENT THROUGH ALL the scant linen in the bathroom, scrubbing the past four days off of me—Rosalie, blood, gore, Thea, all of it swirling down the drain. Then I lay down on top the sheets. I wasn't tired—but come daylight, I would be. Where in here was safe? Could I really count on housekeeping to not open the door? The curtains here were thick—all curtains in Vegas were—but were they completely impenetrable to daylight? I wouldn't know until it was too late.

I only had a few hundred bucks left. I was sure after that I could jack people for more using my voice trick—Rosalie's whammy—but I'd already spent enough of my life scrounging to know I didn't want to live like that. To be forced to continue to seemed unfair.

And on top of all my concerns for safety...I was hungry.

Not *very*. Just a curious tickling inside my stomach—like the fluttering of a butterfly. I was peckish. Not starving, but, I could eat something.

Unfortunately I knew exactly what that 'something' was.

Rosalie's strip club must be the vampire equivalent of owning a shrimp trawler—she could get a fresh haul every night. How on earth would I manage alone without her resources? Especially when I didn't know what I was doing yet?

Rolling over, I saw a bedbug methodically advancing toward me. I sat up, disgusted—then realized we were almost cousins. How was I any different from it?

I—I was still human. Or enough of me was—and a human could make a plan.

I CAUGHT another cab and had it take me to the strip. A lot of the malls attached to casinos had late hours, all the better to shake your winnings out of you. I bought newer, nicer clothing, socks, shoes, and changed into them in a bathroom, coming out a different man. I had visions of going onto casino floors and mesmerizing dealers there into giving me all their money—but there was a reason Rosalie'd used me to keep herself safe. People had eyes and casinos had cameras. When you could live forever, it was probably always better to lay low.

I needed to stay by myself—or go somewhere that was such a blur that no one would notice me. I knew from my tattoo work that the time to practice was not when I was hungry, sad, or had any other pressures happening—it was when I was relaxed and ready, confident but still curious. If what Rosalie had told me was right— the best time to practice was now.

I walked down the strip after that, like I had somewhere to go. Every time I passed another solo person who looked like they could afford it, I came up like I was asking them for directions—and then also asked them with my whammy for a twenty. It proved two things —I was handsome enough to seem harmless and my whammy worked easily in a stress free situation.

I gathered a wad of cash quickly, wishing I'd had the foresight to buy a wallet back at the mall, but at least I could afford a nice hotel room now, one where strangers wouldn't try to break down your door and rob you during the day.

Part of me wanted to revel in my newfound powers. There was a street magician not that far from me, talking to a crowd of people who had their cameras out, doing tricks on a table with cups. When he looked up—for their cameras, not them—he was beaming. I found myself irrationally jealous of him for getting to show off, for not having to take everything seriously—but if he screwed up a trick, no one died. If I screwed up and got too hungry...the weight of everything I'd done at the warehouse, and the way Thea'd been scared of me, came pressing back.

I turned at the next intersection and started looking for somewhere to drink, not knowing if I wanted beer or blood.

It was 2 AM and there was still a line to get into a club. I stood in it, amused by the way that standing in a line somehow proved I was still part of humanity. When it was my turn to get in, no one noticed me telling the bouncer I didn't need ID with my whammy and after that I went inside.

The music was loud and the lights were flashy. I pressed my way through to the bar and ordered a beer. It was Saturday now and a new crop of tourists were in town, intent on draining Vegas of everything she had to offer, while I contemplated draining them. A cluster of girls moved out onto the dance floor as the song changed and I took their spot, leaning my back against the bar and looking out.

There was so much *life* here. Between the bass's artificial heartbeat and the way that people dancing moved, limbs swirling as they soaked with sweat—I could feel it calling. Darker things inside of me woke up and stretched, watching the world outside through my eyes. Each time a girl got too far from her group, each time a man stumbled away alone to pee—something in me kept track of them, waiting patiently for a chance to be released.

"Not a dancer?" asked the man beside me, taking up a station at the bar with his new drink. He was my height, Latino, a little thinner than I was, with piercing brown eyes. His clothing was impeccable, the lines of everything crisp, and he smelled like almonds.

"Hmm?" I said, turning toward him reluctantly. He was too aware, when we were surrounded by so much easier prey. The realization of that—of me thinking like that—made me redouble my concentration on him, shoving the other part of me aside.

"Not a dancer?" he repeated, leaning in.

"Not tonight," I said. I could dance, but I could barely trust myself now, there was no way I belonged on the dancefloor. "You?" I asked, trying to stay focused on him.

"Nah. Crowd's too...." he said, letting his voice drift.

"Young?" I guessed, because all of them looked twelve to me, even though I was only twenty-three. I felt like the events of the past four days had aged me.

He laughed. "Straight."

My eyebrows raised, then I took another look out on the floor, where drunken men and women were grinding on one another. "Yeah," I agreed, and took a sip of my beer. "Aren't there other clubs for that though?"

"Yeah," he said.

"Then why are you here?" I asked, genuinely curious.

"Sometimes I like shitty straight music," he said, with a grin. "And sometimes at the end of the night, people change their minds." The look he gave me then was best described as mischievously challenging.

I knew what he was thinking. And I was thinking that as long as I was talking to him, the other-me that I was scared of stayed away.

"That's a thing?" I asked, accepting his flirt for what it was and trying to return it.

He smiled, took a swig of his beer, and leaned back on the bar. "Oh yeah. You'd be surprised."

I took a swig of my own beer and asked: "Are you turning them gay, or just getting them to excavate their previously unknown gay side?"

"Depends," he said.

"On what?" I asked, turning myself more his way. His eyes flickered over the subtle change in my positioning, then narrowed on mine before answering.

"On them."

I'd looked at men before, but convinced myself it was as an artist, wanting to know more about their bodies, the way they moved. Had that always been true? Maybe he was right. I liked being with women—but at the thought of being with a man—really being with one—things stirred inside me, thoughts that a lifetime lived in Texas had never given a chance to get out.

Temptation pulled hard and I frightened myself. "Well, that's really interesting," I said quickly, like it wasn't interesting at all.

He pulled back a little, knowing I'd rejected his advance. "It is," he said, lightly shrugging one shoulder and returning his gaze to the crowd, searching, just like I had been, for fresh prey. I leaned back too, but found my gaze flickering to him, looking at his slight roman nose in profile, the strong line of his jaw. Being an artist, I'd always had an overactive imagination—it wasn't hard to imagine his lips wrapped around my cock, his brown eyes looking up at me. The thought was a little disturbing—but only because I'd never really entertained it before, nothing else.

And hadn't Rosalie said that I could feed on sex? I'd far rather fuck someone than bite them.

"Hey," I said, before I could lose my nerve.

He swiveled his head back toward me. "Yeah?"

"I think you're right."

His full lips pulled into a grin. "About which part?"

"Not sure yet. Let's go somewhere and see."

He leaned in close enough that I could smell him, underneath his cologne. "Give me a three minute head start and meet me in the bathroom."

Two minutes later, I set my beer on the bar and began walking after him. The line for the girl's stretched out of the hallway, along the back wall of the club, whereas I could just walk on in to the men's. Two guys were there peeing, one was washing his hands, and—just as I was ready to walk back out—one of the stalls opened, the big one at the back. I timed things and snuck in to be with him, unseen.

"This is not what I had in mind," I said, as he latched the door behind me. The music was so loud that even in here we had to stand close to be heard.

"Oh come on, this is probably bigger than the closet you've been living in," he teased.

I snorted. "I'm not—" I began.

"Standing with another guy in a bathroom stall, hoping to get a handy?" he said as he leaned in. I wanted to step back, not because he himself was intimidating, but everything he might represent—he was so sure of himself and, oddly, of me.

"I've never done this before," I said. "I'm not gay. But...." I looked him over, the way his shirt cut to his waist from his shoulders, the way his slacks had a telling sag where he was getting hard. I swallowed. "I'm curious."

He leaned back. "I can work with curious. What's your name?"

And the horror of when I had told Rosalie my name so recently returned. "Jack," I said, softly.

"Jack," he repeated my name just as quiet. "Nice to meet you. I'm Paco."

I nodded. And as if sensing my current fragility he gave me space. "What'd you come in here hoping for, Jack?"

Proof that the world could still matter to me, now that I'd been ripped from its fabric and denied the woman that I loved—even though she might have never really loved me? "I don't know," I said, honestly. "I think I just didn't want to be alone."

Paco's face softened even more at that. "I can work with that, too," he said, and kissed me.

I let him, without kissing him back. I felt his lips land on mine, his tongue stroke against them for entrance, and I opened them for him, feeling him lean against me bodily, pressing me into the cold metal wall behind. He was warm and he was strong, and—having someone close was almost like having someone care. I pressed my head forward, tilting it, pushing my tongue against his, not fighting it but moving alongside it, to taste him as he tasted me.

His hands ran up the sides of my chest, while mine found his waist where his shirt was tucked in—and tugged at it.

"Yeah?" he asked, as he pulled his head back. In answer, I leaned forward, and kissed him again—harder. He made an agreeable sound and his hands went for my belt.

I had one hand wrapped around his waist, underneath his shirt, feeling the muscles moving beneath his skin, and had another pulling his head to mine, as one of his hands started pushing into my slacks. Paco leaned back to chuckle. "No underwear—you're sure you're not gay? Or at least bi?"

I looked down at where his hand was going, feeling him reaching for me. "I was a lot more sure thirty minutes ago."

His hand sank and his fingers brushed my shaft as my cock started to swell, trapped alongside the leg of my pants. "Pretty soon you're not going to be able to turn back."

As his fingers wrapped around me I closed my eyes. "I don't want to."

"Good boy," Paco said, making his thumb and forefinger a ring around me, drawing me up until I was free of my slacks.

Every touch felt electric, like there was a current going through him, through my cock, through me, grounding on the metal wall behind me and then back again as he leaned in. "I'm gonna suck you off, Jack. I want to taste your cum," he said, as he made a broad stroke, and every part of me shivered at hearing the promise in his words.

As he knelt in front of me I closed my eyes, then he pinched my hip. "I'm not some girl down here. Watch," he commanded—and I did.

There are people who think that giving a blowjob is a subservient thing, that only people who are willing to be degraded or depowered, perform them. This is because they have either never given, or received, a proper one.

As I watched the head of my cock go into Paco's mouth and felt his tongue swirl against its underside as his steely eyes looked up, challenging me to try to deny how good it was, being with a man— with him—my hands curled into fists against the metal stall behind me. I heard him chuckle at the same time as I felt it reverberate against me.

He lapped slowly up my shaft, his lips working up it incrementally, like he was working at taking me in—all the while he looked up to watch what he was doing to me. He was enjoying this, this strange taking of my virginity, watching himself conquer my inhibitions bit by bit. And as my cock reached the back of his throat and tilted down, where I could feel him swallow against me—I made a small whine and then felt my fangs start to descend.

We were alone in this bathroom stall, outside the dance went on and urinals flushed, but in here—I could do so many dangerous things to him if he'd let me. I felt an animalistic passion rush through my body, wanting to taste-know-feel all of him at once, not caring if that was through him sucking my cock—or me sucking the blood out of him. I clenched my fists again as his head bobbed, and I tried to regain control.

Paco pulled his head all the way off, stroking me steadily with his hand. "Don't fight it."

I was breathing hard. "You don't even know what I'm fighting."

He drew his lips across the tip of my cock, streaking himself with the precum glistening there. "Just give in," he said, looking up at me, licking his lips, before taking my cock in his mouth again.

I unclenched one fist and brought a hand to his hair, knocking the straight strands out of place, making him look wilder on me. His tongue pulled against the bottom of my shaft with every stroke, rubbing the sensitive part right under my head, then his lips kept his whole mouth tight as he pushed back on. It was good, so good and—

I wanted to come. I needed to come. And he wanted to taste me —I felt my cock get harder as he sped up, sensing the effort I was making to both let go and maintain. He growled to urge me, to own me, I felt the tremor of it even though I couldn't hear it with the dance music right outside and—I clutched my hand into his hair and pulled him onto me and thrust, raising my hips up to meet him just as I felt my balls start to pulse.

His growl changed to a purr of contentment as my load painted his mouth. He took three more long tight sucks and then pulled back, visibly swallowing, still fucking me with his eyes.

"Did you like that?"

I could only catch my breath and nod. "Yeah," I started—yes— but—it wasn't enough. Not like the wave of relief I'd felt after Maya. The need to feed still pressed inside my skin, even worse than it had been before—and I realized my mistake. Me coming wouldn't do anything to satisfy it—it was only the power that someone else released when they did that pushed it back.

I reached down and grabbed Paco, hauling him up and spinning us both so that his back was against the stall, and kissed him hard, tasting the way he still tasted like me. His hands went into my hair and my hands chased down his chest to find skin. I needed to give it to him, and I had to make it good—

My mouth ravished his, kissing him bruisingly hard, and then moved down to kiss other places, the line underneath his jaw, his neck, his ear. I was close enough to him now that I could hear his bloodsong and I instantly knew what it was—the rushing sound inside him that kept speeding up as my hands rose, clawing against the muscles of his chest.

"I want to do things for you, Paco." I whispered I as kissed up. "To you," I corrected. I felt him tense, unused to having control stripped from him—or perhaps from having anyone offer services so earnestly. I pulled back enough to look him in the eyes as I pushed one hand down the front of his pants.

It was my first time holding anyone else's cock. It felt a lot like mine, smooth, and warm, and thick, except that it belonged to him and I could see the way he melted a little as I moved my hand to gently hold it.

"Like what?" he said, his lips parting with a gasp.

"I—I want to fuck you." I knew I meant what I said, and I saw his eyes go a little wide with concern.

"You think I'm going to let you do that here, to me? For your first time?"

"Show me how." The entire time we were talking, I kept stroking.

He looked like he might refuse—and then where would I be, out on the dance floor again, watching solo dancers too intently, the other-thing inside myself waiting to pounce?

"You really think you can...." he began, reaching between us for my cock, finding it hard and ready. "Oh," he said quietly instead.

"Teach me," I said, giving his hand a gentle thrust.

Paco looked at me all over again, as if I were some sort of newly landed alien creature, making a strange request. I kept stroking his cock and thrusting at him softly—then his eyes fell on mine as he decided. "Okay. But only because you want to learn. You promise to be gentle—until I tell you not to be?"

"I do," I said, as he released me and his hands went to his belt to unbuckle it, and then to his fly. Suddenly I could see the very cock I'd been touching, the soft, dark, and lovely skin of it, a vein like a river, rippling down one side. I could see myself sucking it as he'd sucked me, I could almost taste it—but he turned and pushed his pants down, showing me the perfect curve of his ass.

"I don't have condoms," I said.

"Beginner," he laughed, fishing one out of a breast pocket to almost throw at me. I unwrapped it quickly and hauled it on, then waited for further instructions. "Spit on it—get yourself wet—and go slow."

I transferred spit from my mouth to my condomed cock with my hand—and then played my cock down his ass cleft. He made a readying sound and tilted back a little, bracing against the metal wall with his forearms. I leaned forward to kiss the nape of his neck as I tilted myself to fit him and then pressed.

"That's good," I heard him say, and felt his body agree, a wave of relief coming off of him. I pressed my forehead against his back and put my hands over his to push in ever so slightly. "Really good," he went on.

I felt the liquid heat of his body take me as I made my way inside, leading with my hips, until I was hilt deep inside of him, rising on my toes.

"You like that?" he asked.

I leaned forward to kiss him in answer. One of his hands clenched mine—and then we started fucking. We swayed forward and back, his ass eating my cock the same as his mouth had. One of my hands sank to reach for his cock, but he said, "No," so I returned it to the wall, feeling him grind back into me. It was like we were dancing to a song I'd never heard, that I'd only felt inside till now. My breath was on his neck, one of his hands curled back into my hair, the other pressing him off of the stall's wall into me.

"Harder, Jack," he whispered, bracing. I kissed his neck, his ear, his shoulder, and tried to make good, thrusting more strongly. Only the fact that I needed him to come kept me from coming—being in his ass felt just that good. I reached up over us both to grab at the stall's wall with one hand, and then the other, pressing him against it bodily, using the leverage of the wall to pull myself in harder, higher, all the while listening to his blood singing its song to me. He arched himself up, making me go deep, feeling his body tense beneath mine.

"Oh God—right there, Jack—hit me there inside," he said, grinding his ass up. "Keep going."

I yanked an arm down off the wall to grab his waist and pull him closer, not missing a beat in the thrusts I was pounding into him. His cock swung between us, someplace between soft and hard—I didn't know what to do with it, it seemed like he was enjoying this and I was certainly enjoying fucking him—

He curled forward farther, dragging my other arm down off the wall and into his mouth to muffle the sound of a shouted scream—and I knew he was coming, oh God, coming so hard—I could feel his ass take me, squeezing my cock tight and—

Life

—radiating outwards, from somewhere in our hips—*life*—warmth, heat, safety, satiety—*life*—I ignored the way he was biting my arm to stop from screaming as my load flooded deep inside him.

I covered him, panting, pulling slowly back, feeling the tightness of his ass try to keep me in as my cock slid out. Paco's cum was spattered on one of his pant legs and the floor. I moved back to sag against the opposite wall and he turned to survey himself with a relaxed grin.

"Messy—but totally worthwhile."

I caught my breath as I tossed the condom into the toilet. The hunger—it was gone. I felt...practically human again. Far better than I had after I'd fucked Maya—because Paco was human. He'd given me the real thing, not some sad echo of it. I met his eyes. "I think you just saved my life."

His eyebrows rose. "I bet you say that to all the boys."

"No—I mean it," I said, still overwhelmed with the sensation.

"I'm glad. But don't be getting ideas." Paco pushed his cock back into his pants and fastened them up again. "Have a good rest of your vacation, Jack."

And without saying anything else, he was gone, leaving me in the stall alone.

CHAPTER TWENTY-THREE
JACK

As a vampire, I could grift enough each night from tourists and talk my way into a late room at any hotel downtown—the kind of places that you could be sure that housekeeping wouldn't come into your room to see what you had to steal during the day if you put the 'do not disturb' sign up. I changed rooms every other night, always worried that Tamo would find me—or that Rosalie would get peeved and tell him. The nights in between I made sure to feed.

Being with Paco had opened up a world of possibilities. There were just as many women in Vegas looking to hook up as there were men—but in general, men were a more certain thing. And as people like me—people who wanted to top, but were also intently focused on making their bottom come, no matter what, and repeatedly if possible—were apparently something of a rarity, within a few weeks I'd gained a certain notoriety.

Was I happy? It was hard to say. I didn't have anyone else's blood on my hands, or in my mouth, which was good. I derived a certain satisfaction from using my powers as benignly as possible, and having a certain rep amongst that crowd wasn't a bad thing.

But...it wasn't fulfilling either. I turned, as I so often had in my past, to my art—but it was hard to get supplies when I lived an all cash lifestyle, after most stores were closed, and everything on the internet required bank accounts and credit cards. I thought I was getting ahead, while in reality I was in denial. Nothing impressed that on me more than waking up dead-er one day.

I opened my eyes. The world stayed dark, and for a horrifying moment I thought Tamo had found and blinded me. But I started moving a moment after that, and found myself constrained by plastic, which would explain the chemical smell.

I brought my arms up alongside my body, reached up, and found a zippered seam.

I was in a body bag. *Wonderful.*

I heard breaks squeal as the table beneath me shimmied. I was being transported—to where? I couldn't hear anything but muffled sounds of traffic. Better to be loose out here on the highway, then wheeled into an actual morgue. The zipper didn't have a tab on my side of things, but I was plenty strong—I tore the thing open like a trash bag, birthing myself into the ambulance.

"Hey—hey!" shouted a very startled EMS tech sitting nearby.

"*You didn't see me,*" I growled at him with my whammy. I was shirtless, but there was no time to steal his—I ran for the door, opened it up, and leapt out into traffic. I dodged honking cars until I lunged into the bushes at the side of the road.

I found out later the floor of the hotel I'd been in had had a fire requiring an evacuation, which was when they'd found me and assumed I was already dead from inhalation. My only saving grace had been that it'd been near sundown, and they'd put me in the bag before they'd taken me outside.

And now I was just how I was when I'd left Rosalie. All forward momentum—all my cash, my scrounged art supplies—gone.

"What the hell happened to you?" There was irritation in Bruce's voice—along with an aggrieved parental fear.

"I'm sorry." It'd taken me a few weeks to get back to where I'd been before the fire—but I was all too aware of how quickly another quirk of fate could knock me down. I was managing to live from night to night, but I needed something to live for. "I kept meaning to call, but...." I said, remembering when Thea had told me much the same thing. Inertia was a steep slope, especially when you knew you were wrong.

"Leaving me hanging was an asshole move."

"I'm so, so sorry, Bruce," I said, hoping he could hear it in my voice. He sighed into the receiver on his end, his disappointment palpable.

"I thought you were dead."

I frowned into the middle distance, wishing I could explain to him that I mostly was. "I know." I was using a cheap phone I'd bought at a store, sitting on the ledge beside one of the fountain shows behind me.

"So what the hell happened?"

I gave him a fairy-tale version of events, how Thea and I were getting along, we'd moved in together, but it was time for me to earn my keep so she could get off the pole—and asked if he'd mail me my guns.

"You think you deserve them?" he said.

They were mine, I'd bought them free and clear—but I'd left him hanging for rent on the studio above his shop, and he'd probably had to pack all my shit up, even if it was to take it out to the curb. "I hope I do," I said, sounding truthfully contrite.

Bruce snorted on the far end of the line. "Gimme an address and we'll see."

I was nervous about staying at the same hotel for so long, but I wanted to give Bruce enough time to mail me my things. Each night when I woke up at my new and hopefully less flammable hotel I asked the front desk if they had any packages. They didn't—until a week later, when I'd almost given up, and they did.

It was a big box with a Dallas PO stamp. I ran back to my room with it almost shaking before opening it up.

Inside, Bruce had stowed my guns away in their small foam boxes, carefully coiled up all the cords, and had lined the bottom of the box with all my paints, even though the USPS asked you to not mail them. I pulled each one out, setting them in a rainbow in front of the TV.

And last, but not least, Bruce had done me the biggest favor of all —he'd thrown in my color portfolio. Now I could prove that I knew what I was doing, if anyone would listen. I'd still be starting over— but I was getting used to that.

I flipped through the pages, remembering the times, the people, the places. Everything in the box echoed back to a simpler, earlier life, back when daylight was still in my vocabulary, and Thea was in my arms.

But now that she wasn't—I still needed to go out.

It was Friday night and a new club had opened last week. I thought I'd take my chances there before I wound up someplace I already knew, just to see. All the clubs had started blending together, darkness, light shows, fog, mirrors—whatever thematic differences they tried to have, most of them had very similar layouts and décor.

I whammyed my way to the front of the line, peeled off enough cash to make a hooker blush and got myself table service, so that I and a very large bottle of high end vodka could sit near the dance floor, alone.

Between my vampirically enhanced natural charisma and the

lure of free booze, something always broke. Women would notice me watching them eventually, and I could tell by their reactions what they wanted—if they talked to their friends in an alarmed fashion, my gaze moved on, whereas if they were shy and gave me tentative looks—or better yet were boldly interested in dancing for me—I would invite them over.

One such woman was dancing for me right now. Short and brunette with high heels and a higher skirt, every time she tossed her head her hair swung, showing me her delicate neck beneath. At the thought of fucking her my cock throbbed—at the thought of biting her, my fangs pulsed down. I took a swig of a vodka tonic, feeling it lightly burn.

And then my view of her was interrupted by someone both familiar and un. Paco, from a month ago, in the bathroom stall. "Jack?" he said, as surprised to see me as I was him.

"Hey—Paco," I said slowly as if I didn't remember his name, on purpose.

He looked like he was about to say something else, then went with: "Mind if I sit down?"

"Not at all," I said, gesturing to the couch I sat on.

He took a seat, far but not too far away, and his eyes ran over me like they liked what they saw, but then he shook his head deeply. "And to think I figured you for a tourist."

"I used to be. Then some stranger fucked me gay and I decided I couldn't go home again." I gave him a teasing grin.

He laughed. "You're not gay—I saw the way you were looking at her."

I looked back out on the dance floor where the girl was a little confused but still lovely. "You're right. I'm definitely equal opportunity."

"So I've been hearing these crazy stories about some guy named Jack—about him jerking off people in the corners of clubs, him fucking DJs silly inside their booths, and you don't want to know what he's done on top of bars after close, and I thought, that couldn't possibly be my Jack, could it?"

I let my head tilt. "Your Jack?"

Paco ignored me, looking me up and down again. "Nah. Definitely some other Jack."

"Probably. Sounds like some kind of fish tale."

"Yeah, because his cock gets longer with each one."

"What am I up to? I mean, if it were me?" I asked, taking another sip.

"A Louisville slugger."

I snorted, and vodka tonic came out my nose. Paco laughed, and I laughed too, and the girl on the dance floor was gone.

"Well if only someone who had intimate knowledge of my cock could correct them. Someone needs to set the record straight—factual accuracy is important."

Paco acted concerned. "I agree—but—it's been awhile. I wouldn't want to get anything wrong."

I was already imagining all the things he and I could do—I leaned in and gave him a sly smile. "Then maybe I could arrange another viewing?"

"I'd like that," he said, leaning in too.

Without thinking, I kissed him. He tensed up for a millisecond, then relaxed into me and it felt right. I pulled back and found him beaming, so I kissed him again, cupping his head with my hands—as someone behind us shouted out:

"Take it someplace else, faggots!"

I whirled and saw some well-dressed asshole pointing both his finger and his beer at me. I stood without thinking, reaching him impossibly fast, and he drew up, some wiser part of him frightened.

"*What did you say?*" I asked him with my whammy.

"Take it someplace else, faggots," he said, in a much smaller voice, only able to change his volume, but not the words, no matter how much he might like too.

I leaned forward, my eyes narrowing. "Where do you suggest I take it?"

"Outside?" he guessed, terrified.

A girl appeared on his arm, trying to draw him back, just as Paco appeared at mine. A bouncer rumbled up and noticed I'd come from the table behind me. "You're a good customer—we don't want any trouble—"

"Come on, come on, let's go." His girlfriend hauled him away, back into a pack of his preppy friends, while Paco quietly stood at my side. I turned toward him.

"Are you used to that?"

"No. But it's happened before."

"That's bullshit."

"Well, yeah," he said, glancing down.

I stepped up to him and kissed him again, surprising him. He tensed, and I could feel the bouncer hovering. I rocked back and considered starting shit just because I could, then reconsidered.

"We're going," I said, leaning in to snatch the bottle of vodka up off of my table.

"Where?" Paco asked.

"Away from here," I said, giving the bouncer a look that dared him to try and take the bottle from me.

CHAPTER TWENTY-FOUR
JACK

I strode out, bottle in hand, weaving through the crush of people waiting for the bar. "Here," I said, handing the bottle to the brunette I'd been watching earlier.

"Um, thanks?" she said, her eyes bugging out a little.

"You're welcome—you can snag my table if you want—tell them I'll be back."

"Will we?" Paco asked, following me outside.

"Not tonight."

The evening was cool, which was good because I was pissed. Paco gave me a bemused look.

"First time, eh?"

"First time what?"

"That you've had that happen to you."

"Yeah."

"Because you pass for straight."

"Because I'm bi. Which means I'm half-straight, or something." I ran a hand through my hair knocking pieces of it back into place. The way I'd come up on that guy without thinking—and then wham-mied him—it was like a bomb had started ticking inside of me and was still counting down now. I inhaled and exhaled, trying to get back to normal again.

I waved a hand out, not knowing where we were going to go but knowing I wanted the hell away from here. But an Uber pulled in half a block up instead—I saw the guy who'd confronted us inside the club about to get in.

He saw us, too.

He slammed the cab's door and started walking our way. He was with two other friends in addition to his girl and she was already trying to pull him back. One of my hands twitched, and I wished I'd kept the bottle.

"Oh, shit," Paco said, seeing what I was looking at.

"Stay back," I said, putting myself in front of him.

He gave me a sideways look. "I take Krav Maga."

"Fine then, you take the girl." I said, as the first guy lumbered up. I wanted him to take the first swing, so that technically whatever befell him next would be his own fool fault.

"How many assholes you kiss today, faggot?"

And there he went. I grinned wickedly. "What've you got against kissing assholes? Your girlfriend kisses you."

He swung before I could finish my sentence. He was corn-fed, broad-shouldered, no neck, and out of the club he'd wasted no time putting his baseball cap back on. He swung wide, leaving his side exposed—I could've broken his knee, some ribs, bruised a kidney, popped a spleen, but instead I just cold-cocked him. His jaw could've probably taken a normal man's punch—but I was no normal man. Teeth clamped shut with an audible click, luckily for him he didn't bite through his tongue. He went down like a sack of bricks, baseball cap fluttering to land in the gutter.

By then, one of the other guys was trading punches with Paco, while the girlfriend screamed, and the third guy looked really unsure about his commitment to this course of action.

"Let me," I said, and reached over, grabbing the guy about to punch at Paco with one hand, not spinning him by his shoulder, but holding it instead. He started howling as delicate bones crunched and popped and his arm suddenly slumped down, no longer controlled the way it ought to be, since all its muscle's attachment points were sliding down.

I didn't let go of him. I really should've kept the other guy awake to apologize—the girl was crouched over him, crying, and the third friend had that anxious do-something-but-to-scared-to thing going on, like they were dancing in place, alcohol grinding their decision making process to a halt.

"So you're sorry, right?" I asked the guy I was holding, pulling his shoulder out and up.

"Yeah," he agreed, coming up on his toes, his voice rising like I'd kicked him in the balls.

"Then say it."

"I'm sorry!" he said, all one word, in a high pitched moan.

I looked to the uninjured man. "What about you? Are you sorry?"

He nodded, eyes wide with fear.

"Say it," Paco said, getting into the spirit of things.

"I'm sorry."

"Sorry you didn't just get into your cab and leave like sane people? Or sorry that you insulted my friend and I here?" Paco asked. There was an angry weight behind Paco's interrogation, born of a lifetime of indignities—most likely the very things that'd inspired him to take Krav Maga.

"Sorry for both!" the guy pleaded, as the one I'd concussed began to come around.

I looked to Paco—he was still angry, but our work here was done —or was it? I could feel the blood trembling inside the man I held. I could pull his arm off and bathe in the subsequent warm spray of blood, glory in the sheer destruction. For a moment, fever dreams overtook me—and then the man groaned and Paco gently touched my other arm.

I let go of the man's shoulder and felt him hiss in relief and pain, falling backwards a few steps.

"We're going to call the cops!" the girl threatened from beside her stirring man.

"Do. And tell them that a couple of faggots beat your ass."

I turned on my heel, listening for them as Paco followed me, catching him surreptitiously looking back. "They're not following us."

"How do you know?"

I shrugged, and walked on.

PACO FOLLOWED me silently for an entire block. By then we'd regained the crowds of the strip, losing ourselves in them, no one knew who we were, what we'd done. He moved to walk beside me, just two guys out on another night on the town.

"What was that?" he asked casually.

"What?"

"Don't pretend." His eyes squinted and lips I wanted to kiss fell into a frown.

I pulled up short and sighed. "It was nothing, all right?" I needed to get laid. Already parts of me were paying far too much attention to the crowds parting around me, reforming on the other side. The short skirts that showed so much leg, the starched stiff collars that hid such strong necks—

"It wasn't nothing," Paco said, grabbing my arm and pulling me toward him, out of the crowd. "That—all looked like it came natural to you. Where do you take classes?"

My eyebrows rose and I barked a laugh. "The school of hard knocks, or something like that."

"Don't make fun of me," he said.

I was chastised by how wounded he looked. "I'm not," I said more softly. "It's just something I can't explain. Do you want to go somewhere together, or what?" I'd inadvertently been leading us back to my hotel.

Paco's eyes searched mine. "Of course I want to sleep with you. But if that's all you want—if you can't be bothered to tell me the truth—then no, Jack, fuck you."

Tell him the truth—someone I barely knew? Then again—he was the only person in this entire godforsaken city who *wanted* to know. The hook-ups I'd been having were just that—they might as well have been random, a new guy or girl every night. Paco was the closest thing I had to a friend. But there was no way he'd believe anything I told him standing on the Vegas sidewalk at 2 a.m.

"If I tell you something cheesy right now like you can't handle the truth, do you promise to find it funny and charming and still come up to my hotel room in exchange for the actual truth later?"

The look his expressive eyes gave me then culminated in a sigh and a headshake. "Sure."

"Okay. You can't handle the truth—yet." I tried to give him a winning smile. "Come on, let's cross the street."

It wasn't till I'd stepped a few steps out I realized just how badly I was hoping he'd follow me. Ten heartbeats later—mine or his, I didn't know—he did.

"This is swank," he said, looking around at the inside of my hotel room, pulling all the curtains open and I made a mental reminder to make sure they were all closed come dawn. I went ahead and set the 'privacy please' swinger on the door handle as I closed it behind me.

"Thanks."

"Have you been here...this whole time?" I saw his mind doing the math of the nightly rate since he'd met me.

"Not always this hotel. But yeah." I sat down on the bed, watching him pace.

"Are you staying in Vegas?"

"For now." I couldn't think of any other town that I could safely get to and get situated in over the course of one night, much less one where people stayed out as late and were as adventurous as here.

"Then why a hotel? Why not an apartment?"

Because leases needed to be signed during the day? "It's not important, really." Except it was, if I was going to tell him.

"Is it embarrassing? Whatever it is you're hiding from me?"

I inhaled. "Kind of? It's...strange."

The corners of Paco's lips quirked up. "You're secretly an heir to a foreign country, slumming it in Vegas until you get abducted and taken back home."

"No, but that's pretty hot, we should roleplay that sometime." I rocked back on the bed on my arms. "What if...in exchange for not telling you the truth, I let you do whatever you want to me?" If I did, he was bound to get off, and I would reap the rewards.

He turned to stand in front of me and tilted his head. "But what if I fuck the truth out of you?" The look he was giving me—the way his cock was starting to swell in his slacks....

"That's a chance I'm willing to take," I said, feeling my own heat rise in response to his. He sat down next to me on the bed.

"Then we should see where things go," he said, and leaned in to kiss me.

All the desperate times I'd fucked people since being turned, the bathrooms, the bars, the bushes—this wasn't like any of those. It was just as fierce—we twined in bed, kissing one another, hands working away each other's clothing—but it was in relative luxury, of both location and time. I had the whole rest of the night to be with Paco, I could explore everything about him—and he could explore everything about me.

His shirt was open, his chest against mine, as I kissed his neck and had my hands in his pants. I moved around to cup his perfect ass as his hands reached in my pants for me. I stiffened the moment he touched me, then relaxed, thrusting gently, loving the way my cock felt against his palm.

"Get out of these," he said then, letting me go to drag my pants down as I kicked my shoes off the edge of the bed, helping him to help me wriggle free.

"You too," I said, fighting with his shirt, so that I could touch more skin.

He swung upright and yanked it off, half-naked and eager above me, his dark cock swinging down. I reached out for it, to feel it warm and heavy against my palm. He hitched his pants lower, then off, and we were naked atop the bed, lit by one lamp, the city lights outside, and distant stars.

"Roll over, Jack," Paco said, his voice low. I knew then what he wanted—what I'd as much as offered, not that long ago. I turned, but not before hesitating a moment too long. "No one's done this, yet?" he asked.

I rose up on my elbows, looking over my shoulder at him. "I've only been somewhat gay for a month."

"So there's still catching up to do. I'm glad," he said, and reached for my back with his hands. They started at my shoulders, rubbing down, like he knew each muscle's name and home, and I groaned because it was more manly than purring.

"That's nice...." He paused, and traced a design. I never saw the tattoos on my back—sometimes I forgot they were there. "These are...interesting. I wonder if they explain how well you fight?"

"They're not from prison, if that's what you're asking."

"No, they're too nice—I guess that's just another mystery I'll have to fuck out of you." His hands went back to kneading me, paying particular attention to my ass and the backs of my thighs. Underneath me, my cock was throbbing, waiting for I didn't know what—but I tried to be patient, all in good time. By the time his hands came back up from my calves to my thighs and worked their way towards my ass, I did that move I'd seen so many women—and men—do; I arched my ass up toward him, asking for more.

"Yeah?" Paco said.

"Yeah. Anything. Stop torturing me." I reached beneath myself to stroke, but he caught my hand and brought it back out as he lay on top of me.

"Shh," he commanded, and I obeyed.

I could've done—well, anything I'd wanted to. Inside some part of myself was raging, demanding that we fuck how we like to fuck, and who was he to tell me what to do? But the rest of me was curious about this novelty, the sensation of letting someone else drive for once.

He moved down the bed, his knees by my knees, as he crouched over and spread my ass with both hands. I felt the weight shift and the heat of his breath and then—I remembered Thea. Me in the shower with her, trying to know her so intimately that I'd never have to let her go—just as his tongue stroked against my asshole, asking for permission to push in. I shuddered in response, and he did.

"Oh," I said, relaxing into him. He made an agreeable sound, and I felt his tongue play around my rim, an entirely new and unexpected sensation for me. "Oh—Paco." I couldn't help but breathe his name. He was working his way both in and around and the nerves there kept sizzling, telling my whole body that what was happening was delightful and new and my cock got harder as I arched my ass back for him to take more of me.

I moaned as he pulled his tongue out and heard him chuckle. "You like that?"

I was smiling at the mattress, I knew he'd hear it in my voice. "Is it that obvious?"

"Yeah. But I think you're gonna like this, more." I heard the wrapper of a condom come off, and then the bed shifted as he crawled up it to lower himself down. I felt the weight and heat of him as his whole body pressed against my back, felt his knees slide wide to fall to the outsides of my thighs, and felt his hard cock pressed against the cleft of my ass.

"You know what I want to do to you, right?" he whispered in my ear.

I ground my ass up into him in response.

"Good," he breathed, and then reached between us to position himself against me.

I had felt nothing—*nothing*—like that before. The way his cock slowly stretched me, making me feel so good as it occupied space inside, all my nerves beginning to sing, the way he groaned above me as he slowly pushed it in—the sensations were overwhelming, almost dizzying. And then it felt like he hit a switch—

"Oh God," I said, hands clenching in the sheet below us.

"Yeah," Paco agreed, pulling out a little to hit it again, and then keep up a subtle rhythm. "That—that's your prostate, Jack. Right there." He drummed against it with the head of his cock.

I was flooded with pleasure and my hips started twitching of their own accord. I hadn't felt this out of control since high school. "Paco—I," I barely had time to warn him before I came, my cum spilling out between my stomach and the bed. Paco stayed perfectly still over me, moaning with each of my ass's sucking waves. "I—I don't know what happened." Again—not since high school. Jesus—

"Shh," Paco said, leaning forward to kiss my cheek. "Did it feel good?"

"Yes. God yes," I answered.

"And can I keep going?"

He was still hard inside me—and my ass still wanted him to take it. "Please," I said, bobbing my hips to prove it.

"Done," he said, starting to thrust again. I arched my ass up, and felt him thrust faster and—

"Oh God." I wound my hands in the sheets to try to stop myself from coming again so fast—and Paco took that as a challenge, to fuck the cum right out of me. He hauled me up onto all fours and I pressed against him as he went hilt deep and—I shouted out wildly as I shot another load. Without hands touching my cock—without anything but the pressure of him being inside me—it was like I wasn't in control of my own body anymore. As if sensing the power he had over me, he started fucking me wilder, harder.

It was all I could do to brace and take his cock as it owned me, making my cock spill out seemingly endless cum, rocking my entire body with crazed pleasures, making my ass wind tight around his cock. I wasn't a man, or even a vampire anymore, I was just something to be fucked—

I shouted incoherently as another load spewed out. Paco drove himself deep and leaned forward to kiss me. "Are you okay?"

His concern for me was telling and sweet. I focused on him with sex glazed eyes. "Keep going."

He growled then, kissed me one more time, hard, then had his way with my ass. He grabbed hold of my waist, stepped one leg up, and then the other, and then became like a fucking machine, plowing me, hitting that spot again and again. Pleasure spasmed through my body like a wave that kept hot cum jetting from my cock. I felt him speed up, heard him groan and knew with my other-senses that he was going to give me so much *life*—I sagged down onto my forearms, giving my whole ass over to him as he pounded it, until he marked his triumph with a wild shout, hitting my spot that one last time, making me milk him as he milked me, the fluids spurting from my cock now running clear.

Life spiraled out of him, just as hot and voluminous as the cum that'd spilled from me—I could almost feel it take a physical form, like he'd been pushing it inside me with his cock, feeling it take up residence inside the rest of my undead body, like for a moment Paco had given me a piece of his own soul.

I was still breathlessly contemplating this, both the fucking and the philosophy, as I felt him sag against me, his chest against my back, his arms over my arms, his legs behind my legs, and then he slowly slid back and pulled out. He fell to the bed beside me as I crawled to fall forward, trying to avoid the oceanic wet spot I'd created, both of us panting.

Paco looked over at me, his own eyes glazed and reached a hand out. I took it, our fingers twining. "I didn't know a man could have so much cum in him."

My lips parted. I hesitated, and then gave in. "Maybe that's because I'm not a man." He had fucked the truth out of me, after all.

Paco's brow furrowed but he didn't move. "Wha?" he asked, lazily.

I sat up to look down at him, taking my hand away. "I'm not a man, Paco."

"What kind of denial circus are you in? Women don't have prostates, Jack."

"I didn't say I was a woman. I'm—and you're not going to believe this—a vampire."

Paco's eyes went wide and then he laughed. "That's the stupidest thing, Jack."

"It's true." I went on all fours over him, looking down. I'd gotten so much life off of him coming that I wasn't sure I could make my fangs emerge—then I looked down the long expanse of his body, felt the heat of his blood running just beneath his skin, and felt the *urge* come on. Two fangs sliced their way out of my palate, descending behind my original teeth. I didn't have to eat now—but I could.

I opened up my mouth to let him see. He blinked, suddenly wakeful. "What the fuck!" he hissed.

"I told you." I sat back on my heels, and willed my teeth to fade. Thank goodness the life Paco'd given me was thick and deep—because of that, it was easy to succeed.

He rose up on one arm, contemplating me. His eyes were wild, but he wasn't running.

"Are you frightened?" I asked him.

"Should I be? I mean, I assume if you were going to kill me, you would've by now, without bothering to tell me."

"I haven't killed...." That wasn't true, precisely. "I haven't killed anyone in a long time. That thing I said in the stall about you saving my life—I meant it. Good sex—when someone *really* comes for me—it pushes the urges back."

"Well after tonight I hope you won't need to feed for a week," he said, laughing nervously.

"I wish it worked like that." I brought both my hands back to my lap. I'd liked what we'd been when our hands were twined. I wondered when I'd get to be like that again—and if it'd be with him.

Paco tilted his head in thought, making the pieces of his hair that I'd knocked askew sway. "So that explains why you've been a man-whore."

"Yeah."

"What's it like?"

"By and large? Lonely."

"How'd it happen?"

"I'd rather not say."

"Then why're you telling me?"

"Because you're the only one who's asked." I was looking at my hands again, afraid to look back up. What if I saw fear there? Or worse yet, pity?

"It must be hard," he said quietly.

"It is." It was the first time I'd gotten to acknowledge it out loud. Being a vampire—being a slave to the hunger inside—sucked. Maybe if I'd had more warning, or more friends, or even a state issued driver's license...I was sure there were easier ways. But the way I was now felt a lot like being out on the street again, on the run from my own omnipresent hunger and the sun.

"Hey," Paco said, shifting on the bed to be nearer to me. "I know a thing or two about being different. Your secret's safe with me." His hands reached for mine and I dared to look up.

And everything I was worried about seeing wasn't there. It was just the same steady intelligent gaze I'd been curious about a month ago—with just a hint of compassion that bled into a smile. "And no one would ever believe me about this besides. Everyone assumes that vampires are always tops," he said, grinning wickedly, and I grinned back.

"Oh, I can top. I've learned a lot of things since we were together last."

CHAPTER TWENTY-FOUR

"I bet." He pushed himself up. "So how long are you staying here?"

"For as long as it's safe." He didn't need to know there was someone after me.

"Will you still be here tonight?"

"I could be. Why?" Was it worth risking Tamo for?

He rolled off the bed entirely and started picking through the clothing on the floor to find his own. "Because I want to know where I can find you again."

"Why?" I asked with feigned innocence.

He picked up his shirt and gave me a coy grin. "Why do you think?"

I was hoping he was thinking every dark and perverted thing I was thinking right then about him, as he kept getting dressed. I wanted to tell him to stay, but dawn was near. So instead I did the next best thing—the most dangerous thing I could have.

"Here." I fished in my pants pockets till I found my room key and offered it over to him.

He hesitated, after seeing what it was. "Are you sure?"

"Yeah."

"Okay," he said, folding it into his hand and putting it in his pocket. "Tonight? After sundown, I presume?"

I sat up, naked on the edge of the bed. "Yeah. But give me an hour to freshen up first, and maybe corral a housekeeper."

"Sounds good." Paco gave me another private grin, then turned and walked triumphantly toward the door. I watched the way his ass swayed, until he closed the door behind him, and heard the lock snick shut.

I got up, closed all the curtains, and flopped back onto the bed avoiding the wet spot I'd created. There was a new feeling inside me, all fractious and tickly—fear, mixed with hope.

I'd find out if I made a bad decision later. But for now—for the first time in over a month—I just didn't feel alone.

CHAPTER TWENTY-FIVE
JACK

And I didn't find myself alone when I next woke. Paco was there, kicked back in a chair, heels up on the desk, flipping through my portfolio.

I sat up in bed, cognizant of the way my hair fell in front of my face, and how I was naked while he was not. He looked over, saw me sitting, and almost jumped out of his own skin.

"I'm sorry," he apologized.

"What the fuck?" I complained. "I thought I told you to wait an hour." I looked around the room, doing an inventory for other people, crosses, cameras.

"I just...." He put the portfolio down and looked abashed. "It just didn't feel real. I thought maybe I'd come back here and you wouldn't be here at all—or if you were, that what you'd told me yesterday was a lie, or some strange trick."

"Yeah, because *pretending* to be a vampire is what gets me all the guys." I swung my legs out of bed and stood up.

"Are you mad at me?"

"A little. And I still need to brush my teeth and shower." I stalked into the bathroom and closed the door.

What had I been thinking, giving my room card to him? I brushed my teeth and tongue, well aware of the irony that I couldn't get to the teeth that most needed cleaning. If Paco had meant me harm— hell, if he'd been a rogue Catholic—I could've been killed. Or, *unalived*—I didn't know what the word for killing something that was already dead was. I spit the toothpaste into the sink, then cranked on the shower, stepping into the stream.

But who could blame him for wanting to satisfy his curiosity? If our positions were reversed, would I have done anything different?

There was a knock at the door. "Jack?"

"Yeah?"

"Can I come in?"

I leaned against the back wall of the shower, letting the water sheet down me. "Sure."

He opened up the door and then closed it behind himself, trapping the steam in. "I'm sorry." His gaze roamed my body, barely hidden by fogged glass. I liked the weight of his attention like I liked the weight of him, on me.

"Not as sorry as you will be, if you don't come in here," I promised. "Right now."

His lips quirked, he kicked off his shoes, and then he took me at my word, stepping into the shower with me, clothes and all.

HIS WET AND wrung out clothing hung over every vent in the room, while we lay nakedly in the bed with the heater cranked up, twined with each other, learning things now, not just body parts. I found out that Paco was an evening shift security guard, which explained how he could play so late with me, but that he wanted to be something more meaningful, like a cop or bodyguard, hence the Krav Maga. I wanted to make a silly joke about him guarding my body, then remembered Tamo and stifled it.

"What did I look like?" I asked him, after bringing his fingertips to my lips to kiss. He traced the outline of my lips with a forefinger.

"Like you were sleeping. Only your chest didn't move. I didn't touch you or anything, I was too frightened to."

"That was probably wise."

"It—it wasn't gross though. If that's what you were worried about."

I blew air through my lips like of course not, but I had been. To think of all the ways I'd been uniquely vulnerable to Paco these past two days—him seeing me dead had probably trumped them all.

PACO KEPT my room key for the next three nights. I didn't need it, I didn't leave the room, all I needed was him. He delivered himself, an hour past sundown, and the things we did to one another until the edge of dawn—I had never felt so intimately known as a mortal human as I did by him, at the end of that week. On the fourth night, I stopped him as he reached for a condom.

"We don't need those anymore, Paco—vampires don't have STIs."

He paused. We were both naked, he was kneeling on the bed, and I'd been luxuriously sucking his cock.

"I just...don't believe it."

"You saw me dead."

"I know. But when I'm with you—I don't remember that anymore."

I wondered if that was some unknown mind-wiping vampiric skill on my part, or the work of pure emotion on his. I looked up at him from my lower position. "Do you want me to show you my teeth again?"

"Not when you're down there." He reached down and made a show of pulling his cock away from me.

CHAPTER TWENTY-FIVE

"But you do believe me, right?" I asked, and kissed his much less tender knee.

"I both do and don't believe you. It's hard."

"As hard as you?" I asked, reaching out to stroke him, and he purred. "I could always bite you," I teased, but like so many other teases, revealing a hidden truth. I did want to bite him. Not to bleed him or hurt him—but in the same way that I'd eaten out Thea's ass in the shower so long ago. Because I wanted to know him, utterly, completely. My fangs shifted at the thought of it, my ache for his blood becoming a full bodied throb. "Someday, Paco—I do want to bite you. But I want you to want it, too."

He looked down at me for a long second, his thoughts a mystery to me, then gently caught my head in his hands.

"No biting during blow-jobs," he said, and brought my mouth back to his cock.

I SPRAWLED on the bed after he left, the taste of his cum still thick in my mouth, replaying the hours that'd come before—the way he'd pressed me *here*, the way I'd pushed him *there*, the whispers and the groans. This wasn't life as I'd once known it—but it was good, and getting better.

Then there was a knock outside my door. I stood and strode over, wondering if it was some neighbor come to ask us to keep it down—and saw Rosalie and Tamo standing outside. She knew it when I saw her through the peephole.

My stomach instantly filled with acid—what if they'd seen Paco in the hall?

"Let us in, or we'll break the door."

I reluctantly twisted the handle and then stepped back into a crouch at the bottleneck where the room went from hallway to bedroom. "What do you want?" I asked as Tamo stepped in, the scar

I'd left on his forehead rough and jagged. She sighed and waved a hand in the air behind him.

"This room is rather like your home now. Please allow me entrance."

"Why?"

"Because otherwise I'll make you and that would be in bad taste, would it not? Besides dawn's coming, neither of us have particularly long."

"Come in," I said warily, taking a few more steps back.

"I take it you haven't tried to go anywhere private then, hmm?" she said, looking around at the tangle of sheets Paco'd left behind. "No—I doubt you've left this room in a week. Usually, when creatures such as you and I enter private territory, we have to ask. It's the old rules. Gives the prey a fighting chance."

I didn't like hearing the word prey come from her mouth. It otherized the rest of humanity—Paco along with it.

"I half expected to find Thea here—but what I scent is much more manly," she purred the words and I swallowed in fear. "I knew I felt greatness in you, Jack—charisma, matched with a certain amount of moral adaptability. It's why I can't turn Tamo, no matter how much he might like—he's as inflexible as they come, he'd leave a string of limbless corpses in his wake."

As she spoke, she stared at me with her dark bewitching eyes, words falling out of her perfectly red lips. I shook myself out from under her spell. "Why are you here?"

"To congratulate you on not having killed anyone for sixty-three days. That's more of an accomplishment than you know." Her head tilted graciously to one side. "I keep my eyes on the papers and my ears on the ground. Has there been an uptick of indigent murders, drained bloodless in the night? Girls crumpled behind dumpsters with their legs behind their ears? No, and no." She reached up for my chin with her hand and I grit my teeth as she cupped it. "You've learned to make your way in your new world nicely. Almost too much so."

Paco. What did she know about him? I knew I'd tell her anything —everything—if she asked me too with her *voice.*

"I'm just here to make sure you're not getting any ideas, Jack. The nights can be lonely, even for one such as I. For you?" She snorted with mirth and drew my chin down, forcing me to look at her. "If you try to make another vampire I will kill you—after I force you to kill him in the most gruesome way imaginable." She let the threat hover, then grinned as if she'd just offered me candy. "So don't get too comfortable here, okay?" she said, and patted my cheek before dropping her hand.

"Okay," I said.

"Good. And now it's bedtime—for both of us, hmmm?" she said, and sauntered back toward the door, then stopped and turned around. "You still remember what it's like to be human, so you want to pretend to be one. That is a weakness, Jack, but don't worry, it will fade." She smiled at me like that was something to look forward to, then walked out.

Tamo followed behind her—but not before casting me back a knowing look with a toothy grin. He knew where I slept now—and dawn was coming.

CHAPTER TWENTY-SIX
JACK

I raced to the windows—I could feel dawn nearing, a pressure behind my eyes, like a headache mixed with a freight train—and I grabbed the phone to talk to the front desk as I started shoving my few belongings inside a pillowcase. I couldn't get another room in this entire hotel, it was convention season, plus weekend, plus weddings alas and—

"Where can you get me a room?" I shouted into the receiver, standing there, panting.

A sister hotel. Three blocks down.

"Tell them I'm coming—and the room has to be ready when I get there."

I hauled on clothes and tied two pillow cases worth of clothing to the handles of the wheeled luggage that held my guns and inks, and tossed a wad of twenties behind me for housekeeping before running down the hall.

I could see myself inside the elevator—I looked like an indecisive hobo. No, a tweaking hobo, with the way I was pacing, hoping I could get to the next hotel before dawn. I sprang out of the elevator the instant it opened, and started running, my baggage rattling behind.

THE FRONT DESK sensed I was in a rush and found my mannerisms worrying—but between my willingness to pay the actual posted room rate for a week in advance, and me using my *whammy* I got into a new room just in time. The curtains here didn't seem as thick—so I grabbed all the bedding and locked myself in the bathroom, making a nest to sleep on in their oversized tub.

I woke up to my cellphone buzzing at me. Paco—wondering where the hell I was. I blinked at his message in the dark.

It wasn't safe for him to be with me. Not when Rosalie could sic Tamo on me and ruin my life—what little remained of it—at any moment. I flipped my phone over, took off the back and battery, and lay in the darkness with my hunger.

What was I, *really*? Enough light crept in underneath the room's door from the hallway and then beneath the bathroom's door for my other-eyes to see my hands raised in front of me. They looked like human hands—but I knew I could use them to kill another human, almost without thinking. Rosalie was right—I wanted to still be human, because I liked what I saw in Paco's eyes when he looked at me. But how could I earn that look when I was using him to save me?

Was it possible to save myself?

THE FIRST NIGHT wasn't so bad. Just like any night I'd spent with Paco —only without him.

The second night my senses awakened. Even though I had decided not to feed, my body disagreed and began looking for opportunities. The bathroom I hid in was against the wall, and this room was near the elevators, so I could feel footsteps passing and hear conversations. The laugh of a woman, the crying of a child. The room above me ran the shower, I could hear his heavy steps on tile, while somewhere in the room behind me a woman ran a vibrator until she screamed.

It didn't matter how many blankets I hid under, how tightly my hands were pressed to my ears—there was so much life everywhere around me, except for *in* me—it was like life itself was begging me to take it. My stomach churned, eating itself up inside, curling me into a ball.

On the third night I think I began to go insane. What'd started as a hyperawareness of my personal space had gone beyond that—it was like I could feel the entire tower, above and below, breathing. Waiting for me to act. To do *something*. My stomach unwound enough for me to stand, so I did, coming out of the tub for the first time, hands clutching at the marble countertop in the dark.

I—hurt. I hadn't hurt ever since Rosalie had turned me, but now I felt fragile, like if I was brushed wrong I would snap. My stomach roiled, empty, needles of acid stabbing me inside—and not just in my stomach, but up and down my entire body, a thousand separate torturous pinpricks. I turned the light on and jerked away as it burned my eyes, then observed myself as I became accustomed to the light—my cheeks were sunken, my eyes sallow—I knew now I'd look dead if someone saw me in the daytime.

But—I couldn't let it—the *hunger*—win. I had to prove to myself that I was more than this. That I was in control. That whatever Rosalie had put inside hadn't poisoned me eternally.

Somehow I let it convince me that the only way to really prove that was to go out and face temptation.

I MADE my way out onto the strip, grifting twenties—it was a little harder now, as I looked more dangerous, I suspected, with my hunched shoulders and needy eyes—and with the way that I looked at every human I interacted with like I might eat them. I found myself slinking in shadows more and more, I told myself to protect them from me—but I knew secretly part of me liked it. It was easier to watch for someone breaking from the herd in the dark.

I sat down on a bench, knowing there was still probably a camera or two watching—I was in front of the Bellagio, and every inch of the Strip was televised somewhere via assorted CCTVs. I didn't know what I was waiting for, only that each second longer I waited proved that *I* was in control of me. Not Rosalie. Never her again. I clenched my hands into fists at my side, frustrated anew and—hungry. *Goddammit.* Starving. Worse than when I quit smoking cigarettes, aching worse than after the football team had beaten me, unable to think of anything but....

I heard a scream and a splash from behind me. I whirled, and saw everything like the moment was frozen. A mother on a nearby bridge with her hands out stretched, a camera falling from them into the water below—following her tumbling child.

The hunger took over, and in an instant I was chest deep in frigid water, hoisting a wet toddler overhead by the straps of their denim overalls.

"Oh my God!" the mother screamed from up above. Twenty people leaned over, holding out cell phones to film me. "Teddy! Is he all right?"

His screaming said his lungs were fine—it had a tinge of terror, and the way he was twitching—and the way I was paying attention to that—the way I couldn't *stop* paying attention to that—if the water hadn't been so cold as to shock me when I jumped in, the people filming might've filmed something very, very different. I trudged to the edge of the artificial lake handing him up to strangers before pulling myself out.

"Where did you even come from? You're an angel!" Teddy's mother shrieked, pulling me in for a Midwestern hug. "Thank you—thank you!"

"You're welcome," I said, freeing myself from her as quickly as I could, slinking away.

AFTER THAT, I walked, trying not to see anyone around me. My wet clothes and shoes chafed, but that was nothing compared to the growing knowledge that I was going to do something bad tonight, whether I wanted to or not. There was no time to make myself look good and head out to a club, and I wouldn't trust myself to fuck anyone in my current state. I didn't want to fuck-kill anyone accidentally-on-purpose.

I just needed...space. To make decisions. To figure out who and what I was. Before the hunger made them for me.

I passed Excalibur, Luxor, Mandalay, like temples named after forgotten gods. I took a right on Hacienda and left the laughing tourist temptations of the Strip behind for the businesses and warehouses that served them, looking for what I didn't know—until it found me, right outside the Desert Meats processing plant. The irony did not escape me.

A night security guard. Same as Paco, just a different place, a different shift.

"Hey, what're you doing?"

My body was going unerringly toward him. I was more conscious of it now than I had been at the fountain—it was like I was a rider on horse with no reins.

"Stop!" he shouted, reaching for something on his belt, a gun, a radio, it didn't matter—I leapt on him. We fell together to the ground, me on top, on all fours. He struggled, which only made the parts of me I couldn't control thrill in anticipation—

"Stop!" I shouted at myself, just as he shouted it again at me. The shouting, the fear—as he punched me to no avail—the way he wriggled beneath me, the scent of him pissing himself—the *hunger*

194

smashed his head to one side with one of my hands and brought my mouth to his neck.

Only the last vestiges of my humanity stopped me from leaving his neck a bleeding hole—but I bit him nonetheless. I knew redness welled inside my mouth, the taste of copper, the stuff of life itself, more heady than any wine had ever been. I worked his neck with my mouth at the holes my teeth had torn, siphoning it out of him, his breath like a freight train in my ear. His pulse went from a pound to a tremble and—I rocked back over him, mouth open with the height of my fangs. My hunger wanted more but *I* had had enough. Through sheer force of will, my fangs began to retract. His face was glazed, his body shocky. "I'm sorry," I whispered at him. "I'll go get help," I said, without thinking, then realized how impossible that could be.

I knelt again and caught his jaw, twisting his head back so his collar would help staunch the flow. *"You didn't see me,"* I said with the whammy—and as I said it, I knew he'd agree, it was like I was speaking with the voice of God.

"What—who?" he whispered weakly.

I undid his belt and wound it around his neck tight enough to help things clot, but not so tight as to choke him, and then I ran back for the Strip.

"Give me your phone. Now," I commanded the first solo male tourist I saw. They threw it at me, then looked at their hand, unable to comprehend why they'd done so. I dialed 911 and called an assault at the warehouse, then handed the phone back to the man. *"Get over to the Desert Meats plant. There's a man on the ground there—stay with him until help arrives."*

The man stared at me blankly and I wondered if it wasn't working— then he started using his phone to look for directions to help him obey.

I watched him curiously, then realized he'd be one more loose end. *"You never saw me. You don't know why you're going there, but you're compelled. Hurry."*

He stared past me like I did not exist and then turned and ran following the directions his phone began narrating at him. I watched him go, and then I sagged like I'd been punched in the stomach—with relief. The starving pain that'd consumed my body was gone and—now I felt free. Wild. Omnipotent. Unstoppable.

It was a good thing I'd done coke before, or I'd have let the sensation go to my head.

As it was, I shouted, "Goddamn!" and jumped up to punch the air. Tourists parted like the Red Sea, avoiding my clearly drunken antics.

This was what blood was like—how had I forgotten, for almost two months? I'd been so traumatized the night I'd rescued Thea that I thought I'd never wanted to taste it again, but now—I ran my tongue over my teeth and gums, remembering the feel of the guard's pulse quivering beneath me and—oh God, how easy it would be to just become this thing, this wild thing that drank with abandon and did whatever the hell he pleased?

I spun on the sidewalk, staring at everyone else around me, trying to remind myself what it meant to be human—and I knew the only man that could help me was the one man I couldn't see.

CHAPTER TWENTY-SEVEN
JACK

The next night I went out wearing black to an EDM club. I wanted to be in a crush of humanity, one with an entire crowd, and I wanted the music to be loud enough to drown out all my thoughts.

I've learned since then that fate likes to fuck with vampires who get fresh blood.

"You!" Paco spotted me as I walked in, just as I scented him, in the hallway to the club itself. He walked up and fiercely punched my shoulder. "What the fuck? I thought you were dead!"

I didn't rock under his punch, but a mortal man would've. He stared at me in anger, but his face went stony as he realized what he'd said.

"I only knew you weren't because I saw some video of you rescuing some lady's kid on the news this morning. Is that what you've been doing without me?"

"No," I said, my voice low. My whole body was reacting to his presence, the way he smelled, the way I knew his skin would feel if I could only touch it. "I'm going," I said, and turned away.

"Don't you dare," he said, grabbing my arm.

I yanked it away. "Don't touch me," I said, though I wanted nothing more. I was a monster, hadn't I proven it to myself?

He looked wounded. "Jack, what'd I do wrong?"

"You didn't do anything."

"Then where've you been?" He reached for me again and I pulled back, shaking my head.

"Things are complicated, Paco."

He stood directly in front of me, forcing me to look at him. "Other things are, maybe. But not me."

I swallowed. Each time I tried to go, the look in his eyes kept me there. He reached for me again, more slowly, and I couldn't stop him, didn't want to stop him, as he rested one hand on my chest, over my heart, where I wondered if he could feel its unearthly flutter. "It's okay if you bite me."

His words hit me like hail and I pushed his hand away. "No."

"It's all I've thought about since you left—how much I wish I'd said yes when I had the chance—if that would've kept you near...."

"It's not safe to be with me, Paco. I've done bad things—and I'll do them again."

"Jack," he said, chastising me.

"No, let me finish. I die every morning. I need to feed most nights." I stared into his eyes, willing him to believe, wanting him to be the one to run. "I am not alive, Paco. Nothing can change that."

His eyes searched mine. "You're wrong."

I wanted with all my heart to tell him to prove it—because I desperately wanted proof of it. I'd almost killed a guard— I'd been tempted to kill a child. But I couldn't encourage him like that, to make him think there was any way he could keep me—even though I couldn't leave. The only thing I knew for sure is that it was the remains of my humanity that made me hope against hope.

And perhaps seeing that in my eyes, Paco grabbed my wrist and pulled me into the next room.

THE BEAT OBLITERATED EVERYTHING ELSE, just like I'd wanted it to. We were at the back of a wall of people, but Paco pulled me through, snaking us forward until we were in the middle of the mob, people waving glow sticks as lights strobed and fog released, like there were giant laser breathing dragons on either side of the DJ's stage. It was almost impossible not to move, everyone in the room was rocking like the beat was a commandment from God—but I stood still, in the field of people dancing like lunatics, arms waving overhead, screaming their delight at each new twist of a dial.

Paco leaned against me, his body fitting mine, me stopping myself from straining toward him, as he whispered. "You're still alive. I know it," he said, and moved to the side, brushing himself against me.

Nerves lit up like wildfire, up and down my body, and heat flooded my belly. "Paco," I protested.

"I know you, Jack," he said, grinding up against me in time to the beat, pulling his hips to mine. I swayed with him, letting him make my body flow. "You're more alive than I am. Don't you feel it when you're with me?"

I couldn't lie—I did. From the moment I'd first seen him at that bar, him challenging my perception of myself, up through the way I didn't kill that security guard. Without Paco there would've been no one to prove my humanity too, no reason to have held back.

The weight of that realization pressed on me as he did. His lips met mine, and I let myself kiss him ravenously, feeling both my cock and my hunger ache, then I pulled back, pressing my forehead to his. If Rosalie was right and I wasn't human, then I wouldn't feel bad about murdering Tamo. If Rosalie was wrong, and I was still too-human—then I would do what I had to, to protect the man I loved.

"Give me two weeks," I told him, whispering into his ear as his hands slid up my back.

"Why?"

"For me to figure something out. Meet me back here." I stepped away from him, sidling back through the crowd until he disappeared.

CHAPTER TWENTY-EIGHT
JACK

I'm not proud to say I stalked Tamo and then murdered him. Maybe someday I'll tell you how I did it—but for now I'll tell you what I didn't do—I didn't touch a drop of his blood. I made it look like an accident, so much so it almost was one. That was that.

Morally adaptable indeed.

TWO WEEKS TO THE HOUR, I was back at the EDM club. I paid, whammied the bouncer about my ID, and then pressed inside. Whatever DJ was here tonight was a celebrity, the place was already packed and it wasn't even midnight.

I wound through the club, using all my senses to search for Paco. I'd convinced myself when I'd seen him last that it was better this way, if he changed his mind I wouldn't have his phone number to call him, or him mine. But when I'd finished making my way through the entire club floor, upstairs and downstairs and bathrooms too, I would've paid any amount of money to be able to text him.

One hour passed. Another. I stood with my back against a wall, scanning the room, hoping every time someone new came in the door, and being disappointed. By two am I'd felt all the bass drops my heart could take. Something had happened. Or maybe I hadn't gotten to Tamo in time....

Then, through the doorway that lead from the bar into the club, a rush of people left as one, a bachelorette night ending with someone sick—and a few new people came in. I spotted him among them and started shoving my way through the crowd.

The crowd, drunken or high, fought back. I didn't want to hurt anyone so I started shouting, "*Let me through,*" until I made a path that led me to his side. When I stopped, the crowd closed behind me again like I had never been there.

We stared at each other for a few moments as the music pulsed, then I spoke first. "I thought you weren't coming."

"Some of us have to wait in line." He grinned at me and I found myself grinning back. "Did you do what you had to?"

"Yes."

"Are you going to tell me what it was?"

"No."

His eyes narrowed as he thought about pressing, but I thought I saw him remember the answer the last time he'd asked for the truth. "Is it done? All the way?"

"Yeah." I nodded a little.

"You want to...." he let his voice drift, looking at me while shrugging at the crowd behind him.

"I do," I said, grabbing his arm and pulling him in.

We knew the night was long enough to dance like we didn't care. I pressed against him, feeling all of him brush against me before leaning back only to have him follow. Knowing what was coming made each building moment sweeter, made each of our movements both more magnetic and mischievous. I could finally feel the music's purpose and let it take everything else but *right now* away.

And then it swelled and we were pressed against one another tight by the thrashing of the crowd and I felt enveloped in life almost so much as to not need to feed—except I still wanted to. From him. I could think of nothing more beautiful and rich. I looked at him and he looked at me, and as if he knew what I was thinking, he started winding his way out, with me close behind.

We paused after we breeched the crowd. "Where to?" Paco asked, chest heaving at the thought of being with me.

"This way," I said, and pulled left.

This wasn't the same club we'd been at when we first met, but the layout was similar, long winding line for the women's bathroom, and none at all for the men's. I went inside and he laughed.

"Really?"

"Yeah." I hopped up to sit on the sink counter and looked down at him. "You took something from me in a bathroom not that long ago, Paco."

"And now you want to take something from me?" He took a step forward to stand between my knees.

"If you'll let me." We were so close and it was as if I were seeing him through two sets of eyes, the still-human ones that noticed the shy quirk of his lips, the way preparing to smile made his eyes crinkle, and the other ones that could see the way the blood in him reacted to me being near—the fear that trembled the pulse at his throat and the way that movement called me, like a quickly waving hand.

He reached his hands up for my face and I moved with his intent, letting him bring me down to kiss him. Our lips parted at the same time, and kissing him felt like coming home. No wonder I'd had to ask him for permission. His hands laced behind my neck and mine ran through his hair and someone came in and made a disagreeable sound. I lifted my head up and growled, *"Go."* He left without question.

"Wow," Paco said, realizing what'd gone on. "Could you always do that?"

"A little." I watched him realize that I could've ordered him to do anything, at any moment, and I went on before I lost my nerve. "We can't be together, Paco. We can be this, whatever this is—but I can never really be with you. Not just during the daylight, but from night to night. It's not safe for me to stay anywhere too long, with anyone. There's always a chance I'm being watched. It could put you in danger."

His lips thinned then he sighed. "Usually when guys say we can't be together it's because they're an asshole."

"I just wanted you to know. Before we do this—if we do this. It doesn't change anything."

"What's the definition of too long?"

"I'm not sure. A night or two a month?"

"What'll you do the rest of the time?"

"What I have to."

His pulse steadied to a firm throb and I thought the moment lost, but then he said, "All right."

It was ask him to repeat it a thousand times, or take him at his word. I hopped off the sink and our bodies twined, both of us stepping against one another, me kissing him up against the wall. The music took on a new speed outside, frantic, as the crowd shouted, caught up in the electronic rhythm's tribal beat, and I decided to take my chance. I kissed him, hard, then pulled back and felt my fangs descend, piercing through skin as I leaned into Paco, parts of him hard, soft, warm.

I waited for a second, not wanting to push his head to the side— then he caught his hand in my hair and brought my mouth down.

My hunger wanted to savage him, but the rest of me knew far better. My teeth pierced his neck, gentle for all they were sharp, and I heard him gasp as I started drinking. The first taste made my heart soar. Life—given freely from someone who knew what it meant— nothing had ever tasted so good.

I told myself I'd only take three sips, but it was hard—my whole body ached for a fourth, a fifth, to get to the bottom of Paco's sweet red wine. I pushed myself away reluctantly, panting, eager, and hard.

He looked at me while my fangs pulled back, as if trying to understand what I was. "Are you okay?" I asked when I could. Because I'd been gentle, the cuts I'd given him had sealed perfectly back up, it was as if I'd never touched him.

"Kiss me," he said, and I did, smearing the red from my lips all over his own. When he didn't return it, I retreated, and saw him looking faintly shocked.

"I can't believe you like that."

"If you only knew how sweet you tasted, you wouldn't give any to me at all." I smeared my thumb across his lips to clean a smear, bringing it back to my own to lick clean.

"Is that it?" he asked. Our hips were still matched, there was no way he couldn't feel me hard.

"For tonight." I took a step back. I wanted to tell him what he'd meant to me, how being with him had given me a tenuous connection to my humanity, but that would've crushed this moment, and made what I'd said before about not being with him more cruel. What I said instead was, "I think you saved my life again."

He stepped closer, and kissed my lips gently. "Any time."

CHAPTER TWENTY-NINE
JACK

After that, unlife was unlife. I tried to make my way in the world, and eventually fell back into doing tattoos via word of mouth. My hands were steadier than they'd ever been, though I thought I could tell a subtle difference between my skills before getting blood and recently after. Paco and I continued our friendship and I made other friends too, though generally I kept my secret to myself.

Then after a few years on my own I met *her*. At a dive bar of all places, it was like the beginning to a noir detective novel. *She* walked in, and I set my beer down.

There was something about her, an innocence, a radiating glow. It called to both halves of me, the human side that wanted to protect her and the *hunger* that wanted to eat someone so pure just to see how she tasted. Before I could distract myself with other thoughts, she noticed me noticing her and held my gaze for just a second too long.

A girl that good wouldn't be in a dive bar on accident, would she? I didn't think my feeling was wrong, she didn't look like an alcoholic. So either she was waiting for a low class friend, or was looking for a little attention. I pulled out a pen and took up a napkin, and did a quick sketch of her face in profile.

She was beautiful so it wasn't hard—high cheekbones, a perfect nose, hair loose and blonde. And when I was done I walked over to her.

"Hey—I know this is weird, but I just saw you and," I shrugged like it was no-pressure, nothing, and handed her the sketch I'd made of herself.

She preemptively winced, waiting for me to do something so gauche as to offer her a phone number—I stood at a respectful distance, feeling bad for her for having to suffer the rest of mankind.

"Thanks," she said, taking it. Then she looked at it, and I saw her eyebrows rise. "Do things like these get you a lot of play?"

"Sometimes," I grinned. "But I tend to only draw really beautiful women, which lowers my average."

She laughed at that, warm and easy, and I could almost feel her checking out my arms. My hands, with their distinctive tattoos were visible—I braced myself to be judged. When she didn't, I dared a name. "I'm Jack."

"Angela."

"May I?" I asked.

"Only if you give me your pen."

Out of all the times I'd drawn portraits, no one had ever asked to see the pen itself afterwards. I wondered if she would write her number down, or if she'd chuck it across the room to buy herself time for an escape. I sat down, not close, not far, and watched her work.

Angela turned the napkin sideways and started in, turning her profile into a mountainside, her hair into a stream. I watched with delight that I didn't bother to hide—I'd never had anyone try to out-art me before. When she was done, she presented it, and I grinned.

"That was awesome." I took it from her, and recreased the folds with a finger, wondering how she'd react if I asked her to sign her name.

"Thank you."

"You're clearly an artist—please tell me it's more than a hobby."

"It is," she said, and started talking.

SOMEHOW WE BOTH did tattoos and knew some of the same people—we'd never overlapped only because she lived her life in daylight.

And that's what it was about her that I found so attractive, I realized as we continued to speak. With her light tan and her blonde hair, she was like a ray of sunlight—no wonder I was so tempted by her. Eating her would be like eating light itself.

She drew out the end of her drink as I drew out the end of mine, hoping that this was going to become something more, trying to figure out how I could make it so. I was my best self, genuine, debonair, and she was hers—lovely, charming, with the kind of laugh that made you want to hear it again.

And then both our drinks were done and there was a pause. I was two nights out from any sort of feeding and needed something tonight, for the safety of myself and others. I knew all the places I could get sure things—blood or sex—but I wanted *her*.

"Do you want another one? Not that I want to get you drunk, but I do want to keep you here."

I could see her surprise at me being upfront. But unlike the rest of the men in Vegas, I had nothing to gain from subterfuge. She gave it a moment's thought, then said the last thing I thought she would. "Let's go outside."

"Sure," I said, and followed her out.

The scent of her in the air, the ten steps from our table to the doorway, the way her hips swayed—there wasn't a part of me that didn't want to be with her, in her, fang or cock—and as we got two steps outside she answered all my prayers by turning around to maul me, kissing me desperately—as if she needed to feed from me as badly as I wanted to feed from her. We spun in the parking lot, mouths tasting, pushing hands through hair, until I'd moved her without thinking to lean up against my car.

"Careful," she said, as I pressed her into it, knowing there was no way she didn't know I was hard.

"It's mine—and trust me, I don't care."

Her hands were on my chest and everything in me wanted to grab a fistful of her hair and pull her near—it was time to ask.

"Do you want to...." I said.

At the same time she said, "We could...."

We both laughed a little, so full of ourselves as the moon pushed out from behind a cloud—and then something changed.

"I...." she began, pulling back. Sensing the change in her, I made room. "I'm a mom. This isn't what moms do," she said, suddenly shy.

No. No, no, no, no. I wanted to know her light *so badly.* "You sure? I feel like I've slept with more moms than you have."

"I'm sure," she said, and it sounded final, no matter that her hair was sexily tousled and I could still taste her in my mouth.

"Okay. For tonight? Or for forever?" I didn't often chase women —or men—down, there were so many other options that there wasn't a need. And I knew better to get involved with someone who had a kid, they didn't deserve that—but that spark of *life* I sensed in her made me want to be reckless—

"For a really long time that I'm not sure about. I'm rusty and...." She brought her hands up as if protesting her innocence—she needn't have, I believed her.

"You don't have to explain. It's all right." I made myself down-shift forcibly. "You do what you have to do."

"Thank you," she breathed, visibly relaxing.

"Of course." Thea had been right about men in this town. The ones who lived here were working too hard to bother to be decent, and no one from out of town bothered to try. "Do you want to keep talking?"

"I probably shouldn't."

Damn. "Sure. I get it," I moved a little further back, giving her even more space—all the more so because the hunger lurched inside, reminding me I was two nights out. If it wasn't going to be her, I needed to go get busy somewhere else. "This is going to sound awful, but, if this isn't happening—I should probably go finish a friend's sleeve like I was supposed to. You were—and are—totally worth standing him up for, but rent's coming up. If you don't need a ride home or anything, that is. You're tiny—one beer...."

"No, I'm safe to drive." She shook her head. "Do you always tattoo so late?"

"Yeah. I'm up till dawn, most nights." If only she knew. Then the moon came out again and illuminated her, and I realized I'd been wrong earlier—I'd thought she was made for sunlight, but something about her positively glimmered beneath the moon. And so I asked for something I knew I shouldn't: "Can I get your number?"

She looked charmed while I was questioning what a damn fool I'd been. "No," she answered, wise enough for us both. "But," she said, reaching into her purse to pull out a business card. "You can call me here."

I took it. "Thanks, but I have my own friends to give me tats."

"No—I'm offering you a job."

My bemusement turned to mystification. "Yeah?"

"Yeah. It's hard to find good vampires."

"What?" *How did she*—

"You know—people willing to stay up till dawn. Good night artists are hard to find. This way you could have your own station—you wouldn't have to share anymore. And I take a smaller cut of night-time stations, since it's harder to get walk-in clientele—so I could be good for you—and you could be good for me," she said, and my other-sight felt her blood rising as she flushed.

No one in Vegas had offered me honest employment before. I was taken aback by the thought of it. "I see."

"Just think about it? And if you want it, give me a call."

I wanted it all right—in all senses of the word. I grinned at her, then made a show of flipping the card across my fingers before putting it into my back pocket.

WONDERING WHY BELLA DIED AND HOW THE PACK IS INVOLVED? BLOOD BY MIDNIGHT: DARK INK TATTOO BOOK THREE IS OUT NOW.
READ ON FOR A SNEAK PEEK.

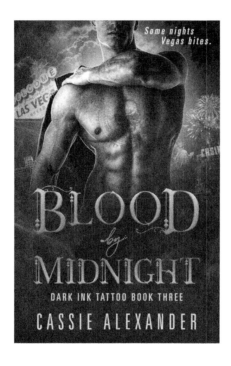

BLOOD BY MIDNIGHT
DARK INK TATTOO BOOK THREE
JACK

I woke up in my own bed, having left Fran's an hour before dawn. Fran was right, Rosalie was the only tie I had to the rest of Vegas's supernatural community, but I was supremely reluctant to call on her. Any time I reminded her I existed she reminded me of the debt I owed her, and if she ever bothered to ask me about Tamo...even though years had passed since his death, discovery still felt like a matter of time. I had no doubt her anger would still be fresh, no matter how long it'd been, even if she didn't find out for a century.

I fed Sugar, took a shower, and did anything else I could think of to do before heading over to Vermillion around eleven.

Due to the circumstances surrounding my creation, I avoided Vermillion as much as possible, a détente that I think both Rosalie and I enjoyed. I was never sure what I was to her—each time I arrived she treated me like a prodigal son, but seemed content to lose track of me for months at a time. Since she always knew where I was,

I knew the freedom I felt was just an illusion, but one that I was glad she seemed careful not to break.

The music was as loud as ever but the place had undergone a remodel—it was shining and clean and lacked the air of desperation that could so quickly perfuse these kinds of places, though I wouldn't put it past Rosalie to mesmerize the last of her patrons every night, turn the lights on, and make them polish tables and sweep floors like some kind of enchanted stripper-loving zombies.

"Jack?" she asked from behind me, a question even though she had to know who I was.

I braced myself, readying an obedient smile before I even turned. "Rosalie."

Her eyes traveled my face, trying to discern the reason I was there. "It's been so long—to what do I owe the pleasure?"

"I have a few questions for you."

One of her perfect eyebrows quirked. "Really? That sounds like you need my help. Can it be?"

My teeth grit shut. It would be putting myself further in debt to her and both of us knew it. So far, I'd been 'working' off my debt by doing occasional jobs for her—because if I didn't, she'd make me. A conquering smile spread across her face, lighting up her dark brown eyes, making her lift her head in triumph, revealing the neck I wanted to bite and then strangle.

"Yes."

She lowered her head again to stare at me. "How badly? I want to hear it in your voice."

"Bad enough that I'm here," I said, flatly.

"True!" she exclaimed, glorying in her power. A girl ran up to her and started talking in a rushed voice while giving me nervous glances. Rosalie cut her short, gave her a brusque order, and then turned back toward me. "Well, Jack, it looks like you arrived just in time."

I didn't ask what for—she turned, and I knew I was supposed to follow.

SHE LED me to the back of the club, which had also been remodeled since I was there last. She pulled me through the room with all the alcoves, each facing onto its own pole, some of them occupied, while the entire group of them faced a currently lonely stage. It was impossible to walk past without remembering Thea. Rosalie looked over her shoulder at me as I slowed down without thinking.

"You're going to have to get better about forgetting the past. Forever is a very long time."

"Have you forgotten everyone you've lost?" I asked before thinking where it could lead.

"I've even forgotten how many I've lost," she said.

"Is that true?"

I could see her considering lying, before deciding not to. "No. But it sounds nice, doesn't it?"

I reluctantly nodded. I didn't want to forget Thea, or anyone else that I'd lost—if I could, I wouldn't be here, waiting to ask her questions about The Pack for Bella. But what would happen when I outlived Paco and everyone else I knew? All the more reason I should be on my own.

We arrived in front of a closed door, although music thumped behind it like a secret heart, and Rosalie fully turned.

"I've got a group of women in and they're getting rowdy—too timid to go watch boys, too hetero as a group to enjoy women. They think they're being risqué, but they were killing the rest of the club's mood, so I threw them in here." She gave the door a dark glance. "I need them to either drink until they're fun or I need to throw them a bone. Yours, to be particular."

"What? No—can't you whammy them?"

Her head tilted, framing her brown shoulder in black curls. "Is that what you call it?" She sounded amused. "Trust me, I'm more experienced at it than you. What happens if I tell them they had fun here? They come back tomorrow night, without knowing why, and don't spend any money again? Worse yet, they bring more friends?"

"So tell them to go."

"I could, but what if that creates lingering negativity that compels them to tell others they had a bad time? The First Seven never had to contend with Yelp."

I blinked. She'd never mentioned the First Seven before—I wanted to ask who they were, but who knew what that would cost me? "Then tell them they were never here at all."

"Ah, I could—but what about cab receipts, drinks charged to credit cards, and photos?" She mocked them, miming taking an imaginary selfie with one hand. "The world's a complicated place, Jack, and I have a business to run. I'd rather take care of their problem organically. With your beautiful, indefatigable organ, to be more precise," she said, and brought her imaginary camera down to pat between my legs. I stepped back before she could touch me, and her nostrils widened at my small defiance. "You are mine, Jack. I let you forget that because I enjoy reminding you, repeatedly, but trust me that the day that I tire of you I will paint the floor with your blood."

The words tripped off her tongue as she smiled and the girl from earlier ran up. She waited to be polite, thinking that she'd interrupted some casual conversation, and without taking her eyes off of me Rosalie put her hand out for what the girl held—a leather collar and a long matching leash. I knew it was meant for me, just as I knew I couldn't escape.

"Rosalie," I said, turning her name into a plea.

She tsked and came forward like she was about to embrace me, buckling the collar around my throat. "You've fed recently, I can tell. You'll be fine." She clasped the leash to the collar's metal buckle as I looked past her at the door. "It's not a lion's den, Jack—and you're not a Christian, besides." She made to tug at the leash and I had a split second to decide if I would obey on my terms or hers.

"And then you'll answer all my questions?" I quickly asked.

"If they leave here satisfied, yes." She turned her back on me and snapped the leash, pulling me toward the door.

Will Jack obey his mistress or find a way to escape her grasp? Keep reading
Blood by Midnight: Dark Ink Tattoo Book Three

And be sure to join Cassie's mailing list for secret scenes, more character art, merchandise, and extra stories!

DARK INK TATTOO SERIES

Don't miss the rest of the Dark Ink Tattoo Series.

...with more to come!

ALSO BY CASSIE ALEXANDER

Check out cassiealexander.com for content/trigger warnings.

The Dark Ink Tattoo series

Blood of the Pack

Blood at Dusk

Blood at Midnight

Blood at Moonlight

Blood at Dawn

Blood of the Dead *(January 2023)*

The Longest Night (Newsletter Bonus Story & Audio)

Edie Spence Series

Nightshifted

Moonshifted

Shapeshifted

Deadshifted

Bloodshifted

Transformation Trilogy *(Coming early 2023)*

Bend Her

Break Her

Make Her

Standalone Stories

AITA?

Her Ex-boyfriend's Werewolf Lover

Her Future Vampire Lover

The House

Rough Ghost Lover

WRITTEN WITH KARA LOCKHARTE

THE PRINCE OF THE OTHER WORLDS SERIES

Dragon Called

Dragon Destined

Dragon Fated

Dragon Mated

Dragons Don't Date (Prequel Short Story)

Bewitched (Newsletter Exclusive Bonus Story)

THE WARDENS OF THE OTHER WORLDS SERIES

Dragon's Captive

Wolf's Princess

Wolf's Rogue *(Coming soon)*

Dragon's Flame *(Coming soon)*

ABOUT THE AUTHOR

Cassie Alexander is a registered nurse and author. She's written numerous paranormal romances, sometimes with her friend Kara Lockharte. She lives in the Bay Area with one husband, two cats, and one million succulents.

Sign up for Cassie's mailing list here or go to cassiealexander.com/newsletter to get free books, bonus scenes, even more character art, and cat photos!